The Stone Buddha's Tears

THE STONE BUDDHA'S TEARS
© 2012 by Somtow Sucharitkul

original published in Bangkok in 2012
by Post Books

reprinted
published by Diplodocus Press, Los Angeles • Bangkok
October, 2013

Second Edition, August 2018

information: diplodocuspress.com

ISBN: 978-0-9900142-5-6

10 9 8 7 6 5 4 3 2 1

The Stone Buddha's Tears

S.P. SOMTOW

DIPLODOCUS BOOKS
LOS ANGELES • BANGKOK

Traditional Disclaimer: Although this novel was inspired by a real incident, the events and characters in it are entirely fictitious. Nobody in it really existed. I made these characters up. Also, I have juggled the geography of Bangkok a little bit so that actual streets cannot be identified precisely. All this, as they say, is to protect the innocent, although it does have the side effect of also protecting the guilty.

to Jay,
who stepped out of a fairy tale
into my world

Contents

The Stone Buddha's Genesis ... an introduction
by the author

The Stone Buddha's Tears

About the Author
Books by S.P. Somtow

The Stone Buddha's Genesis

You're about to read a novel about kids versus establishment, about corruption in high places, about how political expediency can casually upend the lives of innocent people. You're about to read a book in which two young people, a member of the elite and a member of the dispossessed, become friends and work together to bring truth and righteousness to Thailand's fractured society.

So the question everyone will ask me is this: is this book an allegory about reconciliation? Is it a thinly disguised book about a yellow shirt boy and a red shirt boy who become unlikely allies in a battle against common enemies?

Given Thailand's recent history, it is easy to pick up this book and read it this way, especially in view of the fact that some of my blogs have recently been interpreted as favoring one political faction or another. Indeed, I have been vilified by all factions, perhaps a sign that I really have chosen the middle way, the traditional Buddhist path.

But the answer is no. The incident of the wall being thrown up to hide the slum occurred in 1991 and was about showing off the gleaming new Sirikit Centre to the delegates from 160 countries at an IMF conference. 2,000 residents of the Klongtoei slum were displaced and in fact the event was perhaps even more traumatic than the one I invented for this novel.

This book itself was written sixteen years later, around the year 2007, before anybody ever decided to pick sides by picking shirts, and before the current fashion for simplistic answers to complex questions.

It's not about a book about two symbols, two ideologies, two shirt colors, or two classes. It's a book about two boys.

I wrote this novel because I was approached by a woman who had a wonderful plan: to publish a series of children's books, each one written by an author from a different country, which would teach kids around the world something of the daily life of kids in other countries but also not shy away from series social issues. It was a noble idea and at one stage the creator of the series had approached UNESCO as a possible sponsor for it.

Sadly, after many years of trying to set of the series, the various deals fell through and the series producer's option on my book expired, allowing me to seek publication elsewhere. But even then, the book could not find a home; although I've had a number of quite successful young adult books, including the award-winning *Forgetting Place* and the oft reprinted *Vampire's Beautiful Daughter*, somehow a novel of a rather odd length, with protagonists of a certain age, set in a somewhat obscure part of the world did not fit into the publishing plans of any of my editors in New York. My book therefore sat around for years while I did other things, like conducting Wagner and composing new operas.

At length, I realized that the book's journey should really begin in the city that it is about — meaning that it should first appear in Thai. But for a novel whose tone would be hard to capture in translation, walking the fine line between poetry and teenage street talk, I would need a brave translator, one not afraid to take risks. I believe that I have found one in Ngampun Vejjajiva and that the result is more of a collaboration than a translation.

Having said all this it's clear that the book comes from another time, a happier time, perhaps, when one's vision of Thailand's future might have been a little more optimistic than it is at the moment. Implicit in the idea of finally bringing the book out now is my belief that that optimistic time will return, and that through the wisdom of children we may rediscover our humanity and our innocence.

- S.P. Somtow

The Stone Buddha's Tears

Chapter One
What's Your Real Name?

On the one thousandth day of my job as a corner boy at the busiest intersection in Bangkok, I found a wall.

It was a brand new wall, a wall of corrugated iron, the factory-fresh smell of it refusing to meld with the familiar mix of mud, fish sauce, gasoline, and jasmine. It was quite solid. When you pounded on it, there seemed to be no *give* to it. When you put your ear to it, the traffic was strangely distant. In the twilight (the sun would not rise for least another hour) the wall was completely black, steeping the slum in shadow.

In the half dark, others were stirring. A boy named Ake was clambering up a telephone pole.

"Electricity out again?"

"Yeah. Must have ripped out the cords when they put up the wall."

"What's the wall for? I'm gonna be late to work."

"Dunno."

"Well, fix the electricity."

I watched Ake shoot up the pole. It was too dark to see much, but Ake was nimbler than a squirrel. "Got it!" came the raspy little voice from overhead. I looked up. At first I could only see Ake's eyes, glinting against the black spaghetti of electric cabling. A hum. Suddenly, a gray fluorescence stole over the neighbourhood.

I could see my house, a cube thrown together from salvaged boards,   Its latest adornment, a flap over the entrance, was a vinyl banner pilfered from a Skytrain station, advertising a rock concert. Behind the flap, I knew, my little sister was washing her face from a pail that his mother filled every midnight from the tap at the end of the lane, every night when she came home from the factory.

In an hour she would be off to school. Perhaps, one day, I would go again, too. But for now, I had to support my family. There was no other way for us all to survive.

No matter how hard I squinted I couldn't make out where the wall ended. Maybe, when it gets lighter, I thought, I'll see a break in it. A gap where I can bend the iron. maybe.

At that moment, it didn't occur to me to wonder why the wall was there, or who had put it up. Bangkok is a city that is always shifting; buildings come and go; in the slum, with its flimsy building materials, the shifts happen even faster than in the world beyond the intersection. The wall was a new thing, that was all. I hoped it wouldn't stay up too long. It was inconvenient.

I kept going, inching along the crusty metal. This was taking too long. The familiar neighborhood was receding from view. And there were other slim dark shapes now, flitting past ... other kids shuffling to work with the world beyond suddenly blocked from view.

My flip-flops squished through mud now. That was okay. A little dirt was good for business. Looking small and helpless made my life a lot easier. Not just with the clientele, but with the Collector, too. I would clean up in the evening, from the tap on the concrete slab two doors down from my house. Then I'd look respectable. Clean, anyway. No one would guess what I did for a living.

Where would the wall end? I tried to move faster. If I didn't make his quota, the Collector would be angry for sure. I was good at what I did. The Collector rarely needed to correct me, hadn't really hurt me in two years, not too badly anyway.

Not *too* badly, lately. Except once....

As light stole over the slum, the slum ended abruptly in a banana grove. The slum ended but the wall did not end. The grove seemed out of place, a burst of bright green in the half-light.

Furtively, I plucked a bunch of barely ripe *kluay nam wah,* little bananas with seeds, and stuffed them into my shorts. Perhaps I'd be hungry later. You could never tell.

More and more nervously now, pushing up against the wall to avoid being seen, I went on. The mud was caking on my feet. This wall was endless — endless! It was more than an inconvenience now ... I was going to get it. I could already feel it. End now, end quickly, I thought at the wall.

And then, quite suddenly, the wall did end. I came face to face with the side of a tall building. Up and up it went. Suddenly, in the shadow of the skyscraper, it was dark. And strangely cool. But I found what I was looking for — a gap between the metal and the concrete, narrow but quite squeezable. And I pulled myself through.

The street I found myself on didn't look much different from where I worked. Cars crammed the narrow lanes and fumes thickened the air. In the distance, the tops of pagodas peered from behind a shopping center. The tall building whose shadow I stood in was the only such building in sight. Mostly there were shophouses, still shuttered this early in the morning, the shop fronts concealed behind corrugated sheeting, the shop signs a blur of Chinese, Thai, and English.

I know I'd have to double all the way back to find my street corner so I could get back to work. The southbound traffic whizzed by. On the other side of the road there was gridlock. It would probably look suicidal to the tourists who were my best customers, but I just dashed across six lanes of traffic, playing dodgem with the cars that never stopped coming. Why should I have cared anyway?

I started walking, knowing I had to make up at least an extra hour. I wasn't even looking at the people around me, and that's how I found myself walking right into an opening car door.

A sleek white Mercedes had pulled up. The chauffeur was opening the door and I found himself looking into the eyes of another boy.

"Get out of my way," I said. It's never good to scream at rich people, because it makes no difference — rich people always act as if you don't exist. But I was too frustrated to care. I just wanted to get to my corner.

"What cheek!" the chauffeur growled. "Shall I kick him back into the gutter, young master?"

"No." The other boy got out of the car. "That wouldn't be the right attitude to take. And," he added, as the driver shut the passenger door, "you shouldn't call me 'young master' right now."

At last, I saw more than his eyes. The eyes of the rich are usually quite blank. It's as if they don't want to see you, they don't want to know you're there, even when they're interacting with you in some way. This one's eyes were different. They looked right at me. They really *saw* me. Saw more than just another scruffy urchin. I stepped back. It was shocking somehow.

And then I saw him, all of him.

The boy who had emerged from the white Mercedes Benz was a novice monk with shaved hair and a saffron robe. He was very pale — probably never went out in the sun. He cradled a begging bowl under one arm. The hand that clutched the bowl was completely smooth. I looked down at my own hands, chapped and scarred. I was ashamed of them.

"What right have you to go begging?" I told the novice. "Some people really *have* to beg. Leave something for us."

"It's not so easy," the novice said. "Walk with me a while. I'll show you."

"Why would you want me to walk with you?"

"I'm not supposed to *want* anything at the moment."

"So you don't want me to walk with you then?"

"Didn't say that." He didn't talk like a monk. Well, I don't talk to monks much, but you see them on TV sometimes. He sounded like me.

He started walking. He may not have talked like one, but he had the walking down. Not too fast and not too slow. He was going my way, so I shrugged and followed.

No one looked at either of us. On the other side of the street, past the roaring traffic, the wall went on and on. It was covered with murals, children's art, pictures of stick-figure children, playing, dancing. Suns and moons with smiley faces. And as they walked farther I saw an army of kids now, in school uniforms, frantically painting away. What were they doing?

We passed a market, rickety stalls covered with canvas. Tables were set out on the pavement and an old woman was ladling curries and sautéed vegetables from large pots into plastic bags, tying them up with rubber bands. A grinning, shirtless man was carefully arranging the bags on plastic trays, one of each curry, a bag of white rice, a little carton of fruit juice, a bunch of rambutan, a bag of the dessert that looks like little green worms swimming in sweet coconut milk, topped with a little sprig of orchid. People stood in line to buy the trays. We were just in time for the dawn ceremony of feeding the monks.

"What do you mean, it's not so easy?" I said. "There's twenty, thirty people queuing up to give you food."

They came from all walks of life, these faithful alms-givers. There were people in business suits, fine ladies, lads in scruffy school uniforms, housemaids. After paying for a tray of food, they knelt down to doff their sandals; the act of feeding the monks is sacred and can't be done wearing shoes. Any minute now they were all going to converge on the young novice monk and thrust their offerings at him. The novice walked a little more slowly, his eyes humbly downcast as was proper. As if he didn't know what was coming!

But just at that moment, a whole convoy of senior monks popped out of a side alley. They moved as one, with great deliberation. It seemed as though even their breathing was synchronized. As soon as they reached the main road, the line of faithful swiveled around and each one of them picked out a monk to make an offering. The little novice was ignored.

"I told you," said the monk. "You see, giving food to monks collects merit points for your next life. Apparently, they seem to believe that giving food to a grown-up monk ranks higher on the merit scale. A higher merit score, a better reincarnation."

"You'd think that giving to a kid who's too young to take care of himself would get you a higher score."

"Ha! You're what, eleven, twelve, and you're already planning to revolutionize a thousand years of hierarchical thinking?"

"I don't know what you're talking about. I stopped going to school."

"Didn't miss much. What's your name?"

"Boy," I said.

"Oh, but I already have a cousin Boy. What's your real name?"

"Haven't got one."

"C'mon, everyone's got a real name."

"I don't think my parents saw the point."

"You can have mine if you want. I hate my real name. Everyone just calls me Lek. Or

Nen Lek, since I'm having to put up with this novice monk charade."

"Charade?" We walked past a row of shophouses, all selling identical rattan furniture. A row of Chinese medicine shops with their rows of strange-smelling herbs and rocks. No one gave Lek any food. No one noticed either of us. When he got out of the luxury car, when he put on the uniform of the mendicant, he had become like *me.*

"Yeah," Nen Lek said. "It's all politics. You see that fence across the street? That's politics. There's a big international conference in town. They don't want the big international VIPs to see the slum. Urban blight, bad image. No slums on CNN, oh, no, just your shining smiling faces of kids and your gaudy mural ... It's enough to make me ... but I can't. I'm a good little monk."

"Well, at least *you're* not 'all politics'," I said.

Nen Lek laughed a bitter laugh. You know, I never imagined that rich kids feel bitterness. It's the kind of laugh you hear where *I* live, a hopeless laugh that comes from a dark place inside. He said, "My dad's running in the election. He needs an edge. Last time, his edge was a sheet of statistics. It was very clever. I mean, a piece of paper with rows of figures, and you could add them up and see for yourself how corrupt the other side was. But the voters didn't get it. This year it's piety. It's a lot easier to sell. And I'm the poster boy."

"What do you mean?"

"Next week he's having a big press conference. I'll just be out of the temple then, with my hair still shaved," Lek said. "It's a perfect photo-op for the morality vote."

"At least you have a dad," I said, and couldn't quite get the bitterness out of my voice.

"Yeah. I do have a dad." The weird thing was, he couldn't get the bitterness of of *his* voice either.

We walked on longer, in silence, and eventually someone did stop to give Nen Lek food ... two or three people all at once, as we were now several hundred meters past the place where the monks all congregated. The food wasn't all organized on trays, one of each thing ... it was random ... a bag of chips ... a chocolate bar ... mangoes. And a shiny ten baht coin.

"Why don't you take that," he said, "I shouldn't really touch it." A proper, grownup monk who had taken all the vows wasn't even allowed to receive money personally; it could only be handed to a lay person.

I palmed the shiny two-tone coin. I also took a mango. It's wrong to take from monks, but this one was almost a friend. He was saying the alms blessing, his clear high voice ringing against the clang and roar of the traffic. Someone else dropped in a fifty baht note. The young monk looked at it, motioned with his eyes; I stuck it in with the ten. That was a whole morning's take.

"That'll get you off to a good start." That's how I knew he knew what I did for a living. I fingered the coin in the pocket of my shorts.

At that moment, his car pulled up from an alley, and the door swiftly opened. "See you tomorrow," said Nen Lek. And he was gone.

I was only a minute away from my street corner. How far had I walked? It wasn't much for me, but for a chauffeur-driven rich boy....

When he said "See you tomorrow," had he really meant it?

Tomorrow was something I rarely ever thought about.

Chapter Two
The Intersection

There's an alley that connects to the intersection, a narrow passageway, littered with mud-trampled garlands and thick with incense; a Brahma shrine is on the corner and that's why it's so lucky for beggars. It's not the really popular Brahma shrine on the Rajdamri corner, which is clogged with tourists and the hottest begging corner in the city, but it has its share of suppliants.

I'd hoped to slip into position at my corner, but I was too late. The moment I tried to dart to the spot, I saw that the Collector was already there, and before knew it he'd already slapped me in the ear. It was so sudden I didn't feel the sting for a few seconds.

"How many times have I told you, Boy?"

"Too many, sir," I said.

He was in a bad mood. He had his stick out. I thought I was going to get right there in the street, so I waved the fifty in his face. "I wasn't slouching," I said. He grabbed the money and then hit me anyway, but I could tell that he was preoccupied; it didn't hurt much.

"You're a good kid," he said. "But I don't beat you enough."

"No sir," I said, "thank you, sir."

"Who gave you fifty?"

"A monk, sir."

"Ooh, don't lie." He swatted my shoulders. I pretended that it really hurt, squealed as noisily as I could; the Collector couldn't stand embarrassing scenes. "A monk, you say! Now there's a sin, stealing from a monk. You've got a nerve."

"He gave it to me. It was in his begging bowl. They're not allowed to touch money."

"Hypocrisy never ends." The Collector stared at me. I think he suddenly realized I was telling the truth. He went all quiet. It was a bad sign. "You're doing such a good job, Boy," he said, "that I think I'm going to reward you. I'm going to raise you to the next level." He shoved a red tin cup into my hand. A shiny new begging cup. Shinier ... and bigger.

"You're reassigning me to Rajdamri?"

"No, but I'm raising your quota to a hundred a day. Starting today. You've got it too easy. Fifty baht before you've even reached your corner! Obviously I've been letting you off light. Give me a hundred a day."

"But that's not fair. Today was a fluke. They put up this great big fence and I--"

"A hundred baht or a hundred lashes, take your pick." He didn't sound like he was joking. I'd heard the stories about him beating kids to death. Mind you, they were only stories. I didn't think he'd do it to a Thai boy. One of the Cambodians, maybe; they had no I.D. cards; if one disappeared, who would ever know? I only knew that they were bused in from far away, spoke no recognizable language, and were bad for business because they worked longer hours and ate less. "It's not fair," I protested, though not too loudly.

"Yes, but you're almost getting too big to do this anyway. I have to squeeze you while you're still pathetic-looking."

"Can't you get me a job wiping windshields?"

"We don't own that concession. And your contract isn't up yet."

"I know. I wasn't really asking."

"If you can't beg for it, you can always roll another monk for it." He swatted me one more time — for luck, I suppose — and then he was off, loping down the alley and pausing only to scold another beggar before he disappeared around the corner.

I slid into my designated corner, which was in the shadow of a stairwell to a walkway that spanned the intersection.

The walkway connected two huge shopping malls, one crowded and very middle class, the other so upscale that it was practically deserted. The pickings were slim on the middle class side, where I used to work. People always pretended not to see me. If anyone dropped a coin into my can, they always acted as if they weren't really doing it.

But that side of the street had been taken over by another beggars' guild; these were definitely not local; the kids had a scared look, and they didn't speak at all; I didn't even know if they *could* speak.

The rich side should have been worse; the middle class shoppers who crammed into the big mall only *pretended* not to see me, but the rich, well, I think they *really* don't see people like us; we don't even exist. What saves us as we squat in the shadows is the occasional tourist with a big banknote which is nothing to him, but back wherever they come from, he gets to boast about how his insignificant bit of toy money changed someone's life. The worst is when they want to take your photo; you never smile for these photos; you try to look as sad as possible because they give you more for those sad looks; your look of third-world suffering buys them a few seconds of sainthood ... well, in their own eyes at least. Guilt is the great moneymaker when you're working the street.

Under the shade of the walkway, the flower kids congregate. When the traffic gets stuck, they dart in and out, pushing their garlands on anyone foolish enough to meet their gaze. By the Brahma shrine there's a steady traffic in wooden elephants. People come to the four-faced god for favors, but there's always a catch; you have to give something back to the god, you have to make a proper bargain. Wooden elephants make good offerings and after they've been on the altar a while, I think they get recycled. Which is good because it's not the block of wood, it's what it symbolizes.

Well, it wasn't a bad morning. I didn't even have to buy lunch, because some tourists gave me a hamburger. I think they thought it would an exotic treat form me. Anyway, it filled my stomach, along with Nen Lek's mango. I hadn't eaten so much in days, but the long walk around the fence had worn me out. I think that's what made me start daydreaming.

All along the walkway, there were election posters, printed up on vinyl, strung to the edge with bright green twine. I'd never thought about elections before. What did it have to do with me? But I looked at their faces. I can't read that well, but I could see that each one had a number. I wondered which one was Lek's father. There was a huge fat one, a scowling bald one, and another one with eyes that seemed to suck you in; he had gray hair, a mustache, and he was the only one who wasn't smiling. He wore some kind of military uniform and he had the number 9 which is a really lucky number, because when you say "9" it also means to step forward, to make progress. It was a very formal pose. Somehow the eyes looked like they were following you around, staring back at you.

Lek was all shaved, with no eyebrows, but you could see something of him in this man's photograph. Even though I didn't think I'd ever see him again, I lay there on the hot pavement, half in, half out of the shadow of the pedestrian overpass, fantasizing a bit. What was it like to actually *sit* in one of those long white Mercedes? Whenever those rich people's car doors opened, what always hit you right away was the blast of frigid air. The air has its own perfume, too, lemony sometimes, or leathery. They spray the inside of the cars, you see, to keep out the smell of people like us.

At least you have a dad, I'd said to him.

What was that like? Lek's dad was using him as a tool of some kind. How different was that from the Collector, using me to fleece the passersby? Did Lek's dad ever beat him? But Lek's skin was so smooth, so cool, so pale, like the cold air that wafted from his long white car.

The Collector ... I saw him for the first time, a thousand days ago. I know how many days because I count them. It's the one true thing I hold onto. I have to know how many days because that way, I know have eight hundred and twenty-seven days left until I'm free. That's five years, three hundred sixty-five a year plus two leap years.

I wasn't ten yet when I saw him. Our cardboard house had different cardboard. The cube stays the same, you know, but in the rainy season the cardboard shreds to tatters. The logos start to get faint. Fish sauce and beer, tinned essence of chicken, instant coffee, their names all fade into the pounding rain. Corrugated iron is better, but at night, sometimes, the scraps get filched, appear on other houses.

The Collector: lying there dazed in the heat, I saw him the way I'd seen him a thousand days ago. He was a blob of darkness filling the whole entrance to our house. He cleared his throat, and my mother sent my little sister scampering through to the back, where she couldn't be seen.

The Collector said, "School is a waste. He can always go later. But now, while he's small, while he's wiry, while he can scurry through the crowds ..."

He took one step into the house. He didn't take off his shoes. That should have told my mother right away that this man was a law unto himself, outside the rules of society that everyone knows ... even a dirty street boy like me.

I looked at my mother, I mouthed the words, "Look at his shoes."

But she didn't seem to notice. She just said, "I don't want him running drugs or stealing."

And the Collector came all the way in, spattering mud on the one small square of vinyl tile flooring that gave our house the illusion of being a real house. "I'll make sure of that," he said softly. "You'll see, I take care of all of them, teach them the ways, teach them wisdom."

My mother laughed, a short, bitter laugh.

"There are many kinds of wisdom." He reached into the pocket of his shorts and pulled out a wad of thousand baht notes. I think I stared. I'd never seen so much money before. He counted them off. One, two, three, four. He stopped. My mother looked at the floor. She didn't look at me at all.

"What's going on, mother?" I said.

But I knew.

He took me by the hand. He was gentle until we got outside, and then he jerked my arm hard. I cried out. He cupped his hand over my mouth, held me close as though he were hugging me, only it hurt, whispered in my ear, "Don't scream, stupid. Do you want her to change her mind? Don't you know how badly she needs what I just gave her? You scream and you take it all away, all the nice things she needs. I'll teach you not to scream."

He blindfolded me and then I was riding in something, a tuk-tuk I think. And later, I don't know how much later, I was in a room, all concrete, and the Collector was teaching me not to scream. "No screaming," he kept saying, and he kept hitting harder. "Look into my eyes," he said, "and think before you scream. This is for your own good." And when I dared look up at him, I saw there was no anger in his eyes at all; he had a faraway look, like he wasn't even there. It was this emptiness, in the end, that made me stop screaming. It even made the pain go away. Well, not completely. It balled itself up and became all heavy, and it sank and sank, into a dark ocean I never even knew was inside my head.

And maybe that was a good lesson, learning how not to feel.

I looked up at the poster, flapping now in the hot breeze of the cars passing by, and I realized that No. 9's eyes had the same emptiness. They could have been brothers, the rich politician and the lord of the beggar boys.

Later, the Collector had healed me up, rubbed ointment on my bruises, told me again it was for my own good. "A beggar," he said, "should look a little abused. Or how will anyone feel sorry for him?"

And little by little, he taught me the art: the soulful gaze, the pulling at the sleeve, the tear half clenched back. "If I starve you a bit," he said, "you'll learn how to act like you're starving a lot. You may forget, but your body will remember. There's nothing dishonorable about begging. Monks do it. The Buddha did it. Begging well has its own reward." And he slapped me so hard I flew halfway across the room.

Pretty soon I was well enough, and cowed enough, to go out on my own, and I took another blindfolded ride in a tuk-tuk to go back to live in the slum. My mother needed the money I brought in, and my sister had school books.

The Collector ... collected. But he left us a bit to live on. He had kids from all over; the intersection was his turf, all the way up to the edge of the Brahma Shrine. I never told my mother about how I had learned my craft.

Chapter Three
Spreading Compassion

"I waited for you," Nen Lek said. "Walk beside me."

The white Mercedes crawled beside us, the door open. The cold air came pouring out. "It's all right," the novice said to the driver. We were exactly where I had first run into him, but this time, knowing what to expect with the wall, I had started out a little earlier, in total darkness, my red cup tied to my belt loops by a string.

"Just trying to keep you cool, young master," the driver said.

Lek shrugged, and the driver closed the door. He drove on. The novice monk looked ver his shoulder, then pulled me behind a noodle stand. I looked up and saw a man with a camera. He had just missed his shot and he was cursing.

"Who's that?" I asked him.

"Who knows? Maybe it's my dad's people, trying to get candid shots for their press releases; maybe it's the opposition, trying to find an angle to blackmail my dad; maybe it's the press."

"You get followed a lot?"

"They follow me all the time. It makes it hard to keep my vows. Even when I meditate, I think they've got someone watching me."

"I think it's safe now. Shall we go out begging?"

"No, Boy. I've been out a while already. I've got enough." Lek had a saffron-colored tote bag (monks always carried them when they went out) as well as his begging bowl, and the bag was packed. Little rose-scented cakes, a bag of sliced deep-fried bananas, pork skewers in peanut sauce ... but also oddities. There was a ballpoint pen, a bar of soap, and a rattan ball – a *takraw* – which boys enjoy playing with – you can see them in the park – I would, if I didn't have to work all the time.

"I didn't know monks were allowed to play ball," I said.

"We can do what we want," he said, "between meditation and bedtime." He held out the tote bag. "Want anything?"

"I already took money, yesterday."

"But you're hungry."

He was right, but I don't like to be pitied. So I didn't take anything. I just stared. After a while he got tired of holding it out to me, and murmured, "Suit yourself." The more I looked, the hungrier I felt. I palmed the bag of fried bananas. I don't even remember eating them, but they were suddenly all gone. Nen Lek smiled. "Let's spread some compassion," he said.

"Who needs compassion?" I said.

"Everyone," he said softly.

Then this is what he did: he handed me his begging bowl and folded his hands, and he closed his eyes and began to whisper a mantra in a soft monotone. It was weird to see him like this, because around us the crowd was jostling us, more and more street vendors were oozing out of the alley and into the pavement, stray dogs were sniffing, and the cars were streaming past, and yet ... *he* was completely still.

In the churning world around us he had created a bubble of timelessness. And now, he drew me inside it, and I felt sheltered, and cool, not cool like the frozen air conditioning of the steel-glass shopping malls on the corner of Rajprasong, but cool as though a tree had bent its branches to form a canopy over me. I felt I could let go of *everything* and just float. And I did float.

Up above the crowd. Above the skytrain. Above the intersection, where I could see the Collector, scowling, about to cross the street.

Above the wall. I had left myself behind. I saw myself, inside that bubble, smail and frail, with my close-cropped hair and my sunburnt skin and my torn teeshirt.

It lasted only a second.

A car horn. The faint smell of an elephant around the corner.   Then all the noise and bustle all at once, shattering the bubble.   I came back into myself. Nen Lek finished his chant.

"How did you do that?" I said.

"What?"

"You made the whole world go away. Just like that. Only for a second."

"Oh," said Nen Lek, "I didn't think those things worked." He seemed faintly worried, as though something had happened that shouldn't have.

"Do you know what it means?" I asked him.

"It's in the ancient Pali language, the language of prayer.   It's about the waters rushing to the sea ... and compassion spreading out toward all creatures in the universe," he said. "We're supposed to say it when we receive gifts."

"And what's supposed to happen?"

"I don't know.   It's just a formula, just words."   He was totally dismissive, like someone who had heard a lot of words in his life and had learned to believe very few of them. "I never feel anything when I say them."

"I felt something."

"Really?"

"Well ... I don't know." Maybe I had imagined it. But Nen Lek had a wistful look. I think he wanted to believe.

It was a slow day. It was a good thing that my new friend had managed to slip me the small bills that had been placed in his begging bowl, because there wasn't a single tourist all morning, and then, just after noon, something unusual happened. The police came to the intersection. I was dozing off. The heat was really getting to me and there wasn't any action. I woke up to find that someone was prodding me in the ribs with a little stick.

"I.D.," the voice said. I came to right away. You sleep light in this business. I looked around for the Collector. He was supposed to keep the police off our backs. Instead, across the street, I saw that they had nabbed about a dozen of us kids. By their flat and vacant faces I could tell they were Cambodians.

"Hey," I said, "I'm not one of them. I'm Thai."

"Prove it."

"C'mon, officer. I'm speaking to you, aren't I?" I said.

"Could have picked up the language. Give me your I.D."

"I'm under fifteen, sir, I don't need an I.D."

"Student card, then."

"Well, obviously I don't go to school. I've got this job. I have to feed my mother and sister."

"Insolence!" He arrested me. It's no win on this I.D. card business.

Spending the night in one of those facilities usually isn't that bad. It doesn't smell any worse than the slum, and from where I was, I could peer through the bars and see about half of a television screen through an open door where the guards were sitting around laughing. Above the screen was a huge portrait of His Majesty the King.

It's crowded, of course – fifty or sixty in a cell that's meant to hold twenty – but I'm small. I rarely get noticed. They fed me a big plate of rice in a plastic plate and there was even a piece of fried pork that wasn't all bone, and a dollop of fish sauce with chilies. But even the scrumptious smell of fish sauce and chili couldn't mask the smells of the holding cell, the caking sweat, the dried urine. Cockroaches and rats, but I've shared my sleeping space with them all my life; they're like my brothers, I don't mind them.

I knew a lot of the guys in the cell. There was a lot of horsing around, except when one of the guards walked past, rattling his cane along the rusty bars. There were a couple of *farangs,* too, from Europe or America. Usually these sort of people are in for drugs or for bothering children, so I knew to steer clear of them.

I didn't see any of the Cambodian boys, so I assumed they had already been shipped off to the border where they'd have to go through the smuggling process all over again to get back to work. We Thais would have a monopoly for a while. I didn't know how soon I'd get out, but I tried not to think about it. Ever since the Collector had come into my life, I had been drifting along, not really thinking much about any future beyond a day or two away. No reason to stop doing that now.

With my belly surprisingly full, I got sleepy very quickly, propping myself between a kindly old man and a concrete pillar. And this is what I dreamed of....

Flying high above the wall.

The gray walls of this jail. The wall that hid my slum from the sight of the rich. The invisible wall that separated me from Nen Lek's world.

From the sky, Bangkok is beautiful. You see the traffic gridlock but the cars are all shiny, like links in a chain of jewels, catching the bright sun.   The Skytrain and the expressways twist like silver noodles in the

Bangkok air.   Far away, on the river, the Temple of Dawn rises like a forest of upturned ice cream cones.   It's funny that sleeping on a full stomach doesn't weigh me down ... instead it somehow frees something inside me to soar higher. Higher. I've never dreamed in such color. And in my dream there's a kind of perfume, too, wafting through the clouds, a scent of sandalwood, something you'd smell in a temple.

There was a voice, a boy's voice, a voice not yet broken, and the voice was murmuring over and over the ancient words about spreading compassion, and the waters that flow to the sea. Oh, I was soaring.

Oh, and in the sky I saw eyes. Stone eyes that weep.

They woke me up by tapping my shoulder — not lightly — with a cane.

"Wake up, you lucky little cockroach. Someone's bailing you out."

I stumbled into a courtyard, brightly lit; my flipflops had got torn somehow, so every step was gritty and sharp. The guard didn't seem to happy that they were letting me out. I was pushed through another door — it got dark and dank again, very suddenly, when I had barely got used to the light — a narrow corridor, more bolts and locks — and then I was in a white room, where a female policeman behind a table was typing on a computer.

She barely looked up. "Is that him?" she said to someone standing over her shoulder.

He turned. I had barely paid attention to him before — people who work for the rich have a knack of making themselves invisible — but I recognized his voice right away. "Yes, it's him," he said. He glared at me.

Shall I kick him into the gutter, young master?

"Come along, then," he said, adjusting his uniform, not looking me in the eye. putting his cap back on his head.

"Nen Lek sent you? How did he know —"

"Look, I don't know why my master has taken such an interest in you. It can't do any good, this mingling of the classes. You weren't at your usual spot this morning, and the young master thought something bad might have happened to you."

"I'll say. I got arrested."

"For the likes of you, that's not something bad."

He indicated for me to follow, and we were soon walking down some steps towards the waiting white limousine. And then a taxi pulled up to the curb. The Collector got out. He looked at the chauffeur. The chauffeur looked at him.

Something passed between them. They *knew* each other!

The Collector looked at me. Under any normal circumstance he would have cuffed me there and then, but he was curiously subdued. I looked back at him, looked him right in the eye, and in that moment, I didn't quite know how, our relationship changed. The Collector had a look I'd never seen before.

He looked back up at the chauffeur. The chauffeur shook his head, and then the Collector got right back into the taxi. It drove away.

Finally, Lek's chauffeur looked at me. "Don't expect me to the open the door for you," he said.

"I don't."

"And you can't sit in the back. I'm not your servant."

"Wasn't going to."

I climbed in in the front. He started driving. I didn't know where we were going, didn't really care. I was a little scared and a little exhilarated.

"Now listen," he said, "I'm going to drop you off at the intersection where you belong. But tonight, you're to wait by the wall, the place where the wall ends."

"Why?"

"Orders," he said. It was weird that he would do, unquestioning, whatever a little boy's whim dictated. No one had ever obeyed *me*. I wondered again what it would be like to be Nen Lek.

"What's your name?" I asked the driver.

At first he didn't answer me, but then he said, under his breath, "Sombun," and the way he said it made me realize that no one usually ever asked him his name. He was just "driver", the way I was just "Boy."

Sombun was getting onto the expressway and I had never been on it. I stuck my nose to the window, peered into the mirror, and when I saw my own face I recognized the look in the Collector's eyes.

For the tiniest moment, the Collector had been afraid of me.

Chapter Four
The Night Visitor

So there I was, long after sunset, leaning against the far end of the wall that fenced my world off from the real world. On my side, the slum side, the wall was dark. Across the street, there was neon here and there, but it wasn't like the explosive colors of night near the intersection where I worked. Some street food vendors plied their trade, chopping ducks, slicing barbecued pork; a few customers sat in the plastic chairs they'd put out on the sidewalk. Traffic was down tonight.

What was I doing here? All I knew was this — my world had a wall now, and yet in my life, it was as though a wall had been knocked down.   Nothing was certain anymore. I was a street kid who didn't even have a real name, but somehow, I was becoming somebody.

The white Mercedes was pulling up again, and the novice got out of the car. He was putting away a cell phone. He didn't have his begging bowl of course, only the tote bag, saffron colored like his robes, slung over one shoulder. He looked around furtively and I wondered whether he had permission to leave the monastery.

He didn't seem that happy. I didn't even have time to ask him how he was able to be up, out of the monastery, at this hour. I knew the monks go to sleep early. Before I could say anything he said, sulkily, "You weren't there yesterday. I waited and waited."

"I got picked up."

"Do you know what a pain it was to get you out?"

"Do you know what a pain it was to *be* there?"

"Why did you get arrested? What did you do? Did you steal something? Come on, I can fix it. I'll get one of my Dad's people on it."

I realized then that I couldn't be mad at him. He didn't know, didn't have a clue what it was like to be me. "I didn't have to do something wrong to get arrested," I said. "I just happened to be there.   They were clearing the intersection for some reason."

"Yeah. The summit conference. There was a motorcade down the avenue. All the monks were watching it on TV. Big news. Economic boom or something. My Dad knows all about it. He helped arrange it. Still, people don't just get arrested."

It hit me then that my friend, who had waited for me, who had somehow managed to spring me from detention, who had shared his food with me and taken the trouble to sneak out of the monastery to meet me, didn't know anything about me at all. Maybe it wasn't that reasonable, but it made me angry. "You people are all the same," I said. "You see me, see the way I look, you make assumptions. I'm a dirty little street boy, I have to be a criminal."

"Hey, I got you out!"

"Do you want to know what it's really like to be me? I dare you. Spend the night in my house. You'll see."

Nen Lek didn't answer me for a moment. I had the feeling that was weighing many options. Would he be disobeying the Abbott of the monastery? Would he be flouting his father's wishes, perhaps even jeopardizing his father's election? After a long time, he just said, very quietly, "All right." And then he added, "But you're going to have to do the same for me."

"It's a deal."

We didn't shake hands on it, or anything like that, but our relationship changed in that moment.   Because we had just been curiosities to each other before, but now we were in a conspiracy together.   We had secrets. Things to hide from grownups. That made us true friends. Lek turned and, with an imperious wave, dismissed the driver.

I'd walked back through the slum every day of my life for as long as I could remember, but tonight, it seemed like an alien planet.   Maybe it was because Lek stopped to look at the most humdrum things: the electric blue of the plastic drainage pipes, the clothes slung up on wires to dry, crisscrossing over the muddy pathways between the corrugated houses.   Many houses were dark; not everyone was in reach of the stolen electricity.   But even in the darkest hovels there was something going on. An old woman pounding chili paste in a mortar and pestle. A man with an abacus. There was a little shop, too, where you could buy ice cream and tiny packets of shampoo, good for a single wash. And incredibly sweet and salty candies that could pucker your mouth up for hours.   A shirtless old man watched over it but when he saw me with a novice monk he handed me a free ice cream bar.   Then he said to Nen Lek, "I know you can't, but I'll give you something you can...." and he pulled out a bag of cough drops from the back. He offered them lovingly to the boy and Lek said the words of compassionate sharing, and I felt it again, that little moment of utter calm.

As soon as we were out of sight, Lek popped one in his mouth.

"How can you do that?" I said. Everyone knows monks and novices cannot eat after midday.

"There's an exception," Lek said, "for medicines. And these are cough drops."

He gave me one. I sucked on it, enjoying the coolness.

"That man," Lek said, "has been a monk before. He knows about the cough drop loophole. Cheese works, too. In ancient India, in Buddha's time, cheese was considered therapeutic."

"It sounds fishy to me," I said.

"I've learned from my Dad," Lek said, "that no matter what the rules are, there's always a way around them."

That was true all right. Don't *fix* the slum. Just build a wall.

... and it was the strangest night I've ever spent with a friend. Well, in a way, Nen Lek wasn't really a friend at all, but in a way he was more than that. Well, I noticed for the first time what the vinyl banner that was our doorflap really was. It was an election advertisement for Lek's father. Funny how you never see things, never put two and two together. Lek took one look at our doorway and looked at the ground. I think he was ashamed.

But I have to say that when we went inside (and even I and the novice had to stoop, because the door was just an opening cut in the corrugated iron) my mother and sister looked at me with a strange kind of awe. Of course they stared at the young monk as well, but somehow he rubbed off on me. Normally she would have said something about my not coming home for a couple of days. It wasn't that unusual ... there wasn't that much to come home to, after all. I stayed out all night all the time. It wasn't that I was sniffing glue or anything bad like that. Sometimes you just need a change, even if that change means sitting under an overpass all night long, watching the neon lights blink.

"You bless us with your presence, little monk," my mother said.

"Mother," I said, "he got me out of jail." When I said that she looked up at me and she started crying. "No, no, it's all right," I said. "He sent someone down there and even the Collector didn't dare do anything. I'm all right, look, they didn't even beat me up." That set her off even more and soon my sister was crying as well. "What's wrong with you guys?" I was almost shouting at them. I wanted so much for them to be glad to see me.

Then Lek touched me on the shoulder and he said, so softly that only I could hear him, "This is about your father, isn't it?"

I looked away from my mother in shame. I had always been bitter about not having a father, about having to work, about not being able to go to school because the begging was all that kept us going sometimes. But I'd never stopped to think about how she felt about it ... about who my father might have been, what kind of human being he was.

And seeing how the word *jail* had set her off, I suddenly knew.

"Best not to speak of it," Nen Lek said, again so softly that only I could hear. I knew he was right. Because, presently, my mother wiped her tears on a roll of toilet paper that sat on the counter, and she sent my sister to the outside tap to get a bucket of water, and said to my friend, "You've brought back my son."

And finally, with my sister out of the house, she took me in her arms. I felt myself go limp, like a baby, like a doll. I wasn't used to being held. It was queasy, and it was beautiful. And then my mother took a bag of deep fried bananas from the cupboard. "I got these for you," she said. "In case you came back."

It occurred to me that it must have occurred to *her* that I might not have come back. Kids disappear all the time. Especially in my line of work. I try not to think about things like that. But there was a boy in my neighborhood who disappeared once. Someone told me his parents sold him. I didn't believe it.

Food that night was a bowl of rice porridge topped with some flakes of dried shrimp. It really filled me up, especially after the fried bananas. My mother had seen Lek's father on television at the factory. After we ate, Nen Lek helped my little sister with her homework a little; since I hadn't gone to school in a long time, I was never able to help her.

My mother and sister had taken to this boy as though they were his natural family, and I had to admit that I felt a twinge of envy. I knew it was wrong. I mean, he had snatched me out of hell. I stood in the entry and stared at my own family and I felt more alone than I'd ever felt in my life. And I was thinking, there's something inside me, I don't know what, it comes from this desperate way I live, but it's making me want to burst. And maybe I would have burst right then and there but instead the light bulb did. I mean, the only light bulb in our home, the light bulb that hung from the ceiling, that was tied into a cable outside in the alley which stole electricity from the main line. It flickered and went out and we were suddenly in darkness.

It wasn't that dark of course. There were other lights in the slum; electricity was patched a thousand makeshift ways and I saw Nen Lek's and my sister's face lit by the glow of a television that was playing across from them, through the open entry way where the tattered vinyl banner still hung, from the shack of Auntie Nui, who wasn't really my aunt but who worked in the factory with my mother, but somehow managed to keep more of her salary. She was Ake's mother. You remember Ake, he was climbing the utility pole the morning I first met Lek.

My mother took my sister's hand. "Come on," she said, "we're going to sleep at Auntie Nui's."

"What do you mean?" I said. "You can't stand her."

"Maybe you forgot," she said, smilling wanly, "but we only have one bed. It wouldn't do at all."

Monks may not touch women, not even by accident.

"Maybe I should go back to the monastery," Lek said softly.

"No, no, stay, it's nothing," she said.

"Please stay," said my sister shyly.

"Well, they do have rules. I shouldn't be out like this."

"You told me yourself," I said, "they've got a loophole for every rule."

Our bed was a wooden platform with a mosquito net, and a plastic bucket for the necessary. It was a simple thing, and I had never been embarrassed by it before. Lek smiled. "I have a wooden platform at the monastery, too," he said. "My mother was going to send in a bed, but I didn't really want it."

The TV across the alley had changed from a soap opera to the news from the royal palace. You can always tell because the broadcaster switches to the special language they have to use for the royal family. There's a different word for everything, and they're all long, and most people don't understand what they're talking about, but they look grand and they make us feel protected and safe.

I sat for a moment on the plastic stool, hypnotized by the shifting colors. By the time I started to answer Lek, my mother and sister had left.

Later, our dwelling was completely without light. We didn't even have candles. But there was a cold yellow light from the half open entry. It made the mosquito net glow. I lay on the planks, but Lek sat. It seemed that he was meditating. His eyes were closed and his breathing deep and regular. I couldn't tell if he was asleep or awake.

I tossed and turned. So much had happened in the last twenty-four hours, and little of it made sense. I closed my eyes. I might have been asleep. I guess I was dreaming, but the dream was so like the real world that I couldn't tell for sure.

First it's just me running. I've breached the wall somehow and I'm running alongside it. It's night and the sidewalks are jammed with vendors, and around me there's a swirling fog that makes the air sweat with the odors of the night, I mean the jasmine and the rancid fish sauce, the car fumes and the perfumes, the grilled locusts and the garlands. I don't why I'm running except I know I have to get away. I'm being chased and he's gaining ... they're gaining. I don't know who it is. I think it must be the Collector. When the Collector runs, he limps a bit ... it sounds like this ... ta-TUM, ta-TUM, ta-TUM ... but that's also the sound of my beating heart. I run.

I stick to the wall. Schoolchildren who shouldn't be out this late are painting stories on the walls ... they're supposed to be sunny pictures, pictures of happy villagers and smiling boatmen ... but not these pictures. There's a slum house on fire. There's a sad girl in a school uniform under a pink and green neon sign, only I know she's never been to school, she stands there holding out a drink and she catches my eye and says, *Come here, come here,* and in the distance there's a forest of concrete and glass and I run and run and always it recedes and this sidewalk goes on and on forever....

ta-TUM

Someone holds out his arms to me.

Maybe it's my father. That's who I want it to be and I run into those arms and when I look up I see that it's the Collector with his harsh grin and his cold eyes. I struggle in those arms but he holds me tight. I bang my fists against hard muscle. It's harder than I imagine, and my fists are getting bruised and bloody and then I realize that the Collector isn't flesh but stone....

... and then, from somewhere far away, water flows down the stone toward my bleeding hands ... salt water that stings, then takes away the pain ... that pains, then soothes ... and the stone feels cool to me ... like when you're hot and thirsty in the street, begging and baking in the hot sun, and you drag yourself along and then the glass doors of some upscale shopping mall open for a moment to let in some high society matron and the air conditioning rushes out for a moment and touches your skin and takes you to another world ... that's how the stone feels ... it's alive ... and when I look up, I see a face

... a stone face brimming with tears. And around the face the stars are slowly circling.

And I woke up.

I don't know how late it was; three, four. The city hummed. Nen Lek hadn't moved. His eyes were still closed. But I saw that tears were streaming down his face.

"What's wrong?" I said. I sat up. He didn't move. But the tears kept coming, and I saw that Lek's lips were half parted, in a sort of smile. Like he was on the verge of saying something, but he couldn't say it. This was all getting too weird for me; first the dream, I mean, I never dreamed in those days, work just wore me out and I always slept like the dead, and then waking to see the little monk meditating on my bed. "Wake up!" I whispered urgently.

Slowly he opened his eyes. His speech was oddly distant, too, as if were still far away. "I've had the most beautiful *piti*," he said to me.

"What's a *piti?*"

"It's when you break through to a higher state in meditation. A new level of inner emptiness. Oh," he rubbed his eyes with a fold of his robes, "I've been crying. The abbot said that often happens with *piti.*"

"Lek," I said, "I dreamed about a stone face, and the face was weeping."

He looked at me, puzzled. "How? Were you inside my head?"

"I don't know what you're talking about."

"You saw what I saw. What I was trying to see, but I couldn't quite see. It was behind a veil, hidden, but you saw it."

"What?"

"Boy," he said, "you saw the Stone Buddha's tears."

Chapter Five
The Stone Buddha

"But who," I asked him, "is the Stone Buddha?"

So Lek told me the story. He used a lot of long words and he talked about people and places I had never heard of before. He told me there's a buddha image in his temple, and it's kept high up, above all the images, in an inner private vihara, above the images of gold and silver and bronze, because it's an image that came from far away and from an ancient time.

"How ancient?" I asked him.

"It's from India," he said, "from the time of Alexander the Great." I didn't know where India was. I've seen Indians of course. It couldn't be that far away if there were so many people from there on my corner. But

Alexander was an ancient hero; I saw him on a billboard once.   "It's been places, seen things, this statue.   It's been through wars and plagues. It's been in shrines and it's been hidden in a cave and it's been stuffed in a trunk and forgotten, and it's even been in a museum, but it wanted to be here in Bangkok, in *our* monastery; so somehow the statue got stolen from the museum. Sometimes, instead of teaching the dharma, the Abbot gets sidetracked. We love to sneak in a question about the statue. Like, he'll talk about Nepal, and someone will say, 'Was the Stone Buddha ever in Nepal, Lord Abbot?' and he'll smile a little and say, 'Well, it is said that....' and then we'll know, you see, that the dharma hour is going to fly by with some thrilling adventure of grave robbers or corrupt officials or wild animals."

"If it's in a private inner vihara, have *you* ever seen the Stone Buddha?"

Well, soon I will. It'll be Songkran in three days. On that day, we ceremonially wash the sacred images. It's the only day in the year when the public can see it. And once a year something magical is supposed to happen. The Stone Buddha is supposed to weep. So they say."

Songkran is a happy festival. The world is supposed to be renewed.   The last few Songkrans for me were working holidays; people feel more charitable on the New Year;

they throw coins at you as they run through
the streets dodging the merrymakers with
their water pistols and buckets of water.
"Why would a Statue of the Buddha weep on
Songkran?" I had never heard of such a thing,
but who knows, maybe they all did it.

"My Abbot explained. It's compassion for
all the suffering in the universe. They're
supposed to be soothing tears. Cooling your
soul. Like rain, you see. They're healing,
nurturing tears."

Perhaps I would see this miracle. But
more likely I'd spend the Songkran holidays
watching the revelers, trying to see whose
eye I could catch, never really a part of their
world. That's how it had always been.
People like me don't get to see miracles.
Miracles happen somewhere else, to
someone else.

"After Songkran I'll be free," Lek added.
"Dad has his big press conference where he'll
trot me out, and then after the holiday
weekend I can get back to my school work."

It seemed to me that Lek was already
pretty free, but I didn't say anything.

We both got up early; Lek would have to
sneak back into the temple in time so he
could look like he was getting up in time for
his morning begging rounds. This, I
suppose, in a way, dishonest, but I was
learning more and more that truth comes in

many colors, especially for people born to privilege.

On the table, I saw that some food had been laid out: a couple of *khnom sali,* wheet cakes scented with rose, and a few bananas. There was also a little flower garland, the kind you buy from the street kids. There was also a note to me, in childish scrawl (my mother's writing looked even more uneducated than mine) *Offer these properly.* So my mother had slipped back into the house while we slept to leave an offering. I lifted up each gift and folded my palms together and offered them to Lek, putting them into his saffron-colored tote bag which also held his cell phone.

And I thought, ruefully, My mother never leaves *me* food in the morning. But then again, I wasn't a monk.

Lek said, "Go on, eat it all. I have to go on my begging rounds anyway; I can score some more." I stuffed some of the *khnom sali* into my pocket.

We were making our way along the fence. There was moonlight and there was street light leaking into the slum, so we could more or less see our way.

A few meters past my house, I heard a strange metallic grating sound and then there was something in the mud right at our feet. It was Ake. He'd been trying to climb over.

"It's too dangerous," I said. "Why don't you just go around?"

Ake giggled and pointed.

There was now a big gap in the wall. The iron sheet had bent back as easily as as you bend your fingers, and the nails had popped from their wooden posts. We could see cars whizzing by. Ake was getting up, rubbing his behind and spluttering.

"That," said Ake, "is the flimsiest corrugated metal I've ever tried to climb."

"Well, at least we don't have to go all the way to the end," Nen Lek said.

"What, the little monk didn't go home?" said Ake. So he'd heard all about the night visit, maybe from my sister. "Won't the Abbot cane him?"

Lek laughed. "Yeah," he said, "if he finds out."

"It's all right," I said. "He's a friend."

Lek's robes got scuffed as we squeezed through the opening. I followed him through and I saw him rearranging them so that a large tear in the fabric was safely tucked away on the inside. He whipped out his cell phone. "Sombun," he said, "pick me up by the Amporn Shopping Mall, instead of the usual place." He turned to me and said, "Tonight, it's my turn."

I figured I would be spending the night in the temple. I wondered if there would be ghosts. I've always heard that temples have a lot of ghosts.

Ake was staring after Lek. Then he looked at me oddly. "That boy's been on TV," he said to me. "I recognize him even without the hair. My mother watches all the soaps. They bore me, but that kid was in one last year, *The Seven Wives of the Indian merchant.*"

"No. He would have told me." But he probably wouldn't have, I thought to myself. I really knew very little about him.

"How do you know people like that?"

"I don't know," I said. "I bumped into him."

"You try to beg from him? You can't beg from monks. They're not supposed to have anything you can beg. It would be just like you. For that, you'll probably be reborn as a cockroach."

"You're just jealous," I said.

"You're right," he admitted.

The sun wasn't even up yet. "I'm not due at work yet," I said. "I got up early to see him off, and I thought I was going to have to walk all the way around. What are *you* doing up? Don't you go to school?"

"Yes, I do. You might not noticed, but it's Saturday."

He was right. Beggars don't get days off.

"What are you planning?" I asked him. "If you didn't have to get up this early?"

"I'm meeting a friend, too."

"A girlfriend?" With his constant climbing and swinging from poles, Ake was always showing off to the women in the slum.

"Yes." He motioned. Something wet tapped my cheek. I whipped round in shock. Then laughed. It was an elephant. She stood there, filling up the sidewalk, while the first shift of commuters squeezed around her on their way to the bus stop.

"Ladda, meet Boy ..." She wasn't full grown yet. In the twilight I could see that she was covered with wet paint. Someone had drawn designs on her in bold outlines, red and blue and white, the colors of our flag, and she was being ridden by a boy our age. The boy seemed fresh from the country, shirtless and with a *phakomah* wrapped around his waist, and a bright red headband. He was bending down at the moment, whispering something in the elephant's ear. I waved up at him. He only nodded.

"Petch doesn't speak proper Thai," Ake said. "He's from out there somewhere."

"*You* don't speak proper Thai," Petch said in the strange, lilting accent Northerners have.

"Watch it, Boy!" Ake said. Too late. Ladda's trunk had managed to suck the *khnom sali* out of the back pocket of my shorts. I was going to miss lunch after all. They were laughing at me but after a moment I joined in.

"Let's go for a ride."

Ake easily shimmied up the half-grown animal but I had to be pulled up by both of them. The elephant's hide was abrasive; by the time I was sitting between the two boys, I had a couple of raw spots on each arm. I hugged myself and rubbed a bit of spit on the skin, and they laughed again.

"Where are we going?"

"Anywhere she'll take us," Ake said. "but she knows her way around; she knows where the best pickings are." There was a huge bag of bananas slung over the young mahout's shoulder. They were *kluay namwa,* the little bananas with seeds, moist and succulent. My mouth watered.

"Don't touch the merchandise," Petch said.

The elephant seemed to know the way all right. The street was filling up now as the sun began to rise over the distant high-rises. As we moved up the street I could see that the parts of the wall were already in bad shape. Workmen were scurrying to fold the sheet iron back upright. Elsewhere, teams of schoolchildren were at work in their uniforms, touching up their murals of pleasant country life.

The elephant came to a halt in front of a splendid hotel, all marble and glass, with uniformed guards in traditional uniforms including red jackets, gold helmets, and fake-looking swords. She seemed to know exactly where to stop and a crowd of tourists, on cue, came streaming out of the lobby, waving their cameras and their wallets. Ake leapt off the elephant's back with a show of bravado and started selling the bananas. They were feeding her, fawning all over her, rubbing her side and even sniffing her, all the while snapping away on their cameras and mobile phones.

There was a feeding frenzy. The boys helped me off the elephant's back so I could help collect the cash. Ake was charging outrageous sums for the bananas – fifty or even a hundred baht, and they were tossing tips at us for letting themselves be photographed leaning against Ladda or wrapping her trunk around their necks.

"Now I know why you have a TV," I said to Ake.

"We just started this racket a couple of days ago," Ake said. "Petch came down from up north because there's no work for the elephants, they're cutting down on the logging there, thousands of families out of work."

Petch added, "And this is freelance. No gang, no tax paid to a 'collector'. We just pocket the whole thing." Compared to my daily pittance, this was amazing.

"It can't last," I said. "Someone's gonna try to get you into their system."

No sooner had I said that than another elephant crossed the road.   This one was bigger than Ladda, and she was ridden by a burly guy with a goad.   "Hey!" he shouted. "Get off my turf!"

I knew it. "Ake," I said, "the two of you are out of your minds.   These streets are completely controlled.   You're working someone's territory. You could get killed."

The two elephants were now face to face and the tourists were getting confused. The new elephant was well trained. She knelt down on the pavement so that even a child could get on her back.   There was a mini-howdah on her back so two or three tourists could ride at a time. Traffic on the sidewalk was now jammed. Kids were trying to sell garlands, watches, and DVDs to any tourist who wasn't trying to feed an elephant or take a snapshot. Cars were slowing down, too, because while elephants aren't that rare in this part of town, dueling mahouts are worth a look.

"Come on, Ake," I said.   "Attracting this much attention can't be good."

Ake laughed, and Petch laughed, and the two of them couldn't stop and they are cackling like maniacs when the police showed up.   I recognized the one who arrested me two days before. I wasn't going to stay. I slipped into the crowd and found my way to my intersection.

It was a dull day, as far as begging was concerned. It was a hot day, too. When it's hot, people don't take the time to throw in a coin; they want to rush right by you, rush into the coolness of the shopping mall, that hotel lobby, that restaurant. I did collect enough money, but when I handed it in, the Collector didn't glare at me, didn't scold me, barely even looked.

In the late afternoon, Sombun showed up at the usual corner. When I got into the car, Nen Lek threw me a pile of clothes. "You'd better put these on," he said. "You're going to need camouflage."

They were the most expensive-looking clothes I'd ever held in my hands. They were all famous brand names, not the fake versions you can buy on any street corner. I just stared at them and Lek giggled. "They should fit," he said. "And don't worry, I've got lots of clothes. They'll never recognize them."

I wondered who *they* was going to be,

We were going farther and farther from the downtown that I knew. I knew that Lek's temple has located quite far down the road from where the slum was, but that it was all the way straight down; so I was surprised when the car turned up a ramp, stopped at a toll booth, and was barreling down an expressway.

"We passed your temple," I said.

"I know."

"So where are we going?"

"Wait and see," Lek said softly. He fiddled with a fold of his robes and closed his eyes, meditating perhaps. He sort of smiled a little. There was something mischievous about it.

I knew there'd be more adventure tonight.

Chapter Six
Family Secrets

On the expressway, we flew for a long time above a landscape that felt all too familiar to me ... the gleaming tall buildings clenching strips of slumland, the pagodas poking up between dingy apartment blocks, the brown threads canals stitching it all together. Then I saw something I'd never seen before except on television. The urban sea was thinning out, and there were more and more patches of green. Then there was more and more green and less and less concrete, and finally there was a lake, and in the middle of the lake there was an island, and on the island there was a house.

Sombun left the expressway. There was an alley bordered by shophouses. At the end of the alley the Mercedes turned and there was a high brick wall and a gate, and looking back you couldn't see any houses at all; the wall and the trees hid the outside world from view, while ahead of us was a narrow road lined with trees, and it led to the edge of the lake, and from there to a causeway to the island. Soon would come sunset.

I looked back, out of the rear window, and I realized for the first time that you couldn't see any other houses. The place we were going to could have been the only house in the world. Oh, I knew they were there, hidden behind walls and trees, but there was an illusion of total isolation.

"Didn't you put the clothes on yet?" Lek said impatiently. "I'll have to do your hair, too."

I snaked out of my shorts and pulled on soft denim jeans. They covered up a few scars on my legs. I felt self-conscious about the scars for the first time. Then I put on a designer shirt. Again, I couldn't believe how soft it was.

"And now we're going to brush that slum out of your hair," Lek said, and he really had a go at my hair with a stiff wire brush, yanking out the tangles, pulling so hard that it hurt. "And a dash of cologne wouldn't hurt," he added, whipping out a bottle and squirting me with it.

"Stop it," I said, "I feel weird." The fragrance filled the car.

"It's only external," he said, sounding exactly as if he was repeating some lesson learned in the monastery. "Beautiful clothes, beautiful face, it's all on the outside." He told me to stuff my real clothes into the seat pocket and that someone would "deal with it" later. "Actually, we might as well throw them in the trash," he added. "You could use new clothes."

"And how much begging do you think I'll get done if I look like this?" I said.

"True." He looked at me thoughtfully, straightening my collar. "We won't throw them out, then. Tomorrow morning you can change right back."

"Is this your house?"

"One of them," he said.

On the other side of the causeway, the house had a façade of marble columns and there were statues of naked farangs bordering the gravel driveway. I stared at them. They looked so real you'd almost think they were about to come to life. "Who are those people?" I asked him. "Aren't your parents embarrassed to have statues of naked people in front of their house?"

"Oh, those are just Greek gods," said Lek. "My dad collected them from Europe. They're supposed to be naked."

"What are Greeks? Why do they worship naked people?"

"I don't know," said Lek. "Now, try to look dignified, and don't say anything. Just do what I do."

We walked past the spirit house, where someone, a maid maybe, was praying with incense sticks in her folded palms, to the steps that led up to the front porch. The door opened by itself and there was a man in a tunic and turban who bowed to Lek and to me. Lek didn't acknowledge the bow, so I didn't either. I sailed right past him as though I were born to it. Lek chuckled.

The foyer of the house, like the exterior, was all marble and had more of these naked Greek gods standing around. Some of them had wings, and one of them was a woman with no arms. I wondered why they'd put a broken statue on display like that, and whether one of the servants had dropped it while trying to move it. Oddly, it was still really beautiful ... maybe even *because* of the fact that it had no arms. She reminded me of Auntie Prae, the old woman who has the evening begging shift right at the base of the skytrain escalator. Not because Prae was young and beautiful as was this statue, but because she always looked at me with love in her eyes. This piece of stone had the same look of love.

"This way," Nen Lek said. "I'll show you my room."

He started to lead me towards a sweeping staircase. A plump woman in a Thai silk dress came down the stairs. "Lek, Lek," she said, "you didn't say you were coming."

"I'm sorry, mother," Lek said. "Look, this is my friend Boy, from school." I felt extremely awkward as she looked me over. I was so embarrassed I forgot to *wai.*

"Boy," she said, nodding. I am sure she was wondering whose son I might be, whether she was supposed to remember which of Bangkok's upper class families I belonged to. I knew my face just didn't look right.

But Lek said, "You don't know his family, mother. He's from, ah, from Singapore."

"Oh, you'd be one of the hotelier families, then. There's several in your school, aren't there? I do so love the Kuoks," she said. "And don't forget to give Mr. Ho my love next time you're in Orchard Road."

Amazingly enough, we had managed to get away with it. Lek's mother began prattling on now about things I couldn't really understand. "Tonight's not the best night," she said, "your father's got one of those business meetings, he would love them to just *glimpse* you this evening so I think it's all right to see you here, but I'm running off to play cards at your Auntie Kiki's house, and the cook's prepared absolutely *nothing,* and

... do you mind home cooking, Boy? We've nothing fancy today."

"He's shy, mother," Lek said. "I'm sure he'll love the food."

Lek's mother breezed away in a flurry of perfume. Lek turned to me, laughing. "It works! It totally works!" he said.

"So why am I here?" I asked him.

"Because," he said, "I need to find out something. Now come upstairs. I'm going to meditate."

People who have money always keep a *hong phra* in their house, a room for all the sacred images. In Lek's house the *hong phra* was on the top floor, quite a climb, and the house went from marble to wood. The room smelled of incense and perfumed water. Yellow candles burned. Along the far wall was a series of nested altars. On the lowest rung were some faded black and white photographs which looked very old, and they were in gold frames. Some of his ancestors, maybe. Then there were some images of the Four-Faced Brahma and other divinities, and above them all there was a very old Buddha made of wood. The features of the statue were severe, angular, not soft like modern Buddha images. He was standing, and in his outstretched hand someone had placed a flower garland, the kind kids like me sell on the streets. Rotting, the garland gave off a sweet, intense odor. We sat on the floor. There was a rug in front of the altars and it was so soft it sucked my knees right in.

"So, Boy," said Lek, "it's true I'm not where I'm supposed to be. My dad has made a huge donation to that temple, so they'll probably never scold me, and I don't think the Abbot would dare use his cane on me, though heaven knows I deserve it sometimes. But I want you to understand this. I really do try to be good."

"Why are you telling me this?"

"I think maybe you just think I'm being nice to you so I'll feel good, or not guilty about being rich, or something like that. And you know as well as I do that if it weren't for these yellow robes, you and I would never have spoken to each other. But I want you to know ... I think you're happier than me. Sometimes I wish I was you."

"You wouldn't last a day, being me," I said.

"Maybe not. Well, time for me to be good now. I am going to meditate. Do you want to meditate with me?"

"I don't know how."

"Come on, try." He eased himself into the lotus position. "I know you have a gift for it. Because you got into my dream."

"You mean the Stone Buddha?"

"Yeah. Now do what I do." It wasn't hard to get into that position; it's not much different from a begging position, really. But then he asked me to breathe deeply, and to think to myself, as I breathed in, the syllable *bhud-* and as I breathed out, the syllable *dho,* with a long drawn-out *o* sound that's like freeing all the air out of your body. This was hard because I had to do it over and over and over until it seemed that I fell into another rhythm, something outside myself ... as though the whole world were a living, breathing thing and my breathing was just a little fragment of the world's breath.

In my whole live I'd never dreamed I'd be sitting in a millionaire's Buddha room, learning how to breathe. We sat there. It was hard to know how much time passed, because there wasn't any time after a while; time itself seemed to be just another illusion, just as, we're taught by the Buddha, the whole universe is an illusion.

My eyes were closed. The world should have been all dark but it wasn't. At some point, I don't know when, light had begun to steal in.

I was floating in an ocean of light and I could feel that Nen Lek was close to me. I could almost reach out and touch him with just my thoughts alone. Here, on this other plane, he and I could truly be friends. We could let go of it all — the wall between our kinds of people — the richness and the poverty.

I floated.

And finally, in a time that was outside time, I could feel, without seeing them directly, that the eyes of the Stone Buddha were gazing down at me, and I knew that tears were streaming down my cheeks, but I could not really feel them; I was far away from myself.

Boy.

Abruptly, it was over. I snapped out of it. I wiped my face with my sleeve.

"They're calling us for dinner."

Dinner was at a really long table in a marble room where every clink of spoon or glass resonated. Lek's mother and father sat at opposite ends, and Lek and I sat in the middle, opposite each other, as this supposed "home cooking" was being served. Well, it was home cooking in a sense. I mean, it was just an ordinary *phud thai* that you could from any noodle vendor in an alley, but it was served no a huge silver platter. On either side, carrots had been carved into spiraling patterns, and long red chilies had been sliced into wispy flowers that were scattered along the sides of the dish. The noodles were crowned with a cucumber sculpted in the shape of an open lotus.

I knew Lek's father, of course. No. 9 from the big flapping vinyl banner. He looked exactly the same. In fact he looked as if he were always trying to resemble the portrait on the banner. It was hard to not stare because I'd never seen a person from a political banner in the flesh.

We all had individual bowls of lemongrass soup with gigantic shrimp floating in it; you could have fed my whole family on one of those shrimp, chopped into little bits and fried up with garlic and rice.

I didn't even know how to eat this food, and I couldn't watch Lek. Monks of course cannot eat after noon.

Still, he had a little platter in front of him. It contained some slices of cheese, and six cough drops.

Lek didn't eat.

"You're being so good, dearest," his mother said. "But it's all right, you know. The press haven't managed to come out here yet. Would you like me to get some of yesterday's tiramisu from the kitchen?"

"Mother, no."

"Well, perhaps your little friend would like some...."

She smiled at me. I smiled back. I didn't dare say anything.

"I told you, mother, he's from Singapore."

A bad idea, because the lady launched into an incomprehensible speech in some other language. I think it was English.

I nodded, and in English, as I've heard many tourists do, said, "Yes, yes, yes."

Lek's eyebrows shot right up and he could barely suppress himself. I knew I'd put my foot in it. But Lek only said to his mother, "Oh, mother, you know he's just being polite."

She waved and the maid brought me a bowl of what she called *tiramisu.* I tasted it. It was some kind of farang dessert. It was really sweet. Thai desserts are never that sweet; they always have a bit of salt to temper the sugar. Not this. I felt a rush to my head. I wasn't sure if I was going to faint.

At that moment the Collector came into the dining room.

I dropped my spoon with a clatter onto the marble floor. No matter; some valet or butler swooped down and retrieved it, and rushed away to the back of the house while another maid put another spoon down on my place mat.

The Collector looked at me. I don't think he recognized me — not *yet* at any rate. He was preoccupied. He went right up to Lek's father, who didn't motion him to sit. Obviously the Collector's social standing didn't permit him to sit at Lek's table.

Instead, he knelt down and sat in the very respectful *phabpieb* position about two meters from Lek's father, putting his hands together in a self-deprecating *wai.*

"Boss," he said, "it's not going as smoothly as we hoped, but it *is* going." He pulled out a brown paper bag. "Here's the receipts from the district. What's left of them."

Lek's father hefted the bag.

"Seems light," he said.   "You're not cheating me, are you?"

"No more than the usual, boss," said the Collector. "But those votes are getting pricey in your district. They don't like the fence."

"If they vote for me, I can lose the fence, as quickly as I put it in."

"Ooh, Daddy," Lek said, "I didn't know *you* were the one who put up the famous fence."

"Lek," said his father, "when you get out of the monastery, remind me to give you my little talk on deniability. I give it to everyone who works for me, and you may be only twelve years old but what you're doing certainly qualifies as work."

They were the first words I'd heard his father address to Lek all evening.

Lek's mother said, "You'd better go to bed, darling. You'll have to get up at four if you want to get to the monastery before anyone notices."

I had had enough. I was glad when Lek beckoned to me and I was able to get up and leave this uncomfortable dinner.

But as I left I couldn't help looking at the Collector, and he happened to glance up, and I think that, in that minute, he *knew* me. Perhaps he couldn't place me.   He was bewildered.   He looked away.   Once again, just like at the police station, I felt I had power over him.

But what was he afraid of?

Chapter Seven
Spies Like Us

The impressive staircase with the marble balustrade was just for show. Lek showed me a back stairway. The steps were wood. We went up three flights and a low door led to Lek's little kingdom. He had a bedroom, a sitting room, and, accessible by ladder, a loft that was piled with stuffed animals, robots, and gaming consoles.

In the bedroom was a bed that was even softer than the rug in the Buddha room, and might have been as wide as my entire house. In front of the bed was a flat TV screen. Lek switched it on and it was blank at first, but then there were some fuzzy shapes and strange, echoey dialogue.

"I don't know why you went into a monastery at all," I said, "when you have all this to come home to."

"Look, my parents may not take the monastery thing seriously," he said, "but I do. I didn't ask for it — my dad wanted the publicity shots — but it's okay, it really is."

"But you keep sneaking out," I said.

"Okay, I break the rules," Lek said, "but my heart's in the right place." He kept fussing with some controls and suddenly what was on the TV came into focus.

"It's your father!" I said.

Indeed, it was the dining room, and I could see Lek's dad and the Collector, still in his submissive position, and they were conversing in whispers.

"I rigged it up months ago," Lek said, chuckling. "The camera's in a vase. They're fake flowers, so they never think about changing them. I watch them all the time. It's usually boring, but tonight we're gonna learn something."

I didn't know what we could learn, and the whispering was to indistinct for me to make out, but Lek watched, concentrating really hard, as I'd seen him to when saying the words of compassion for all beings. As he watched, I saw his expression gradually change into something I'd never seen in him before. It was rage. No the flinging things around the room kind of rage but something cold and a little bit scary. I backed away from him and didn't say anything.

Finally, Lek said, "My Abbot told me once, that everything in the universe is connected to everything else. You know, like in *Star Wars.* They call it the Force, and we call it karma. My dad is a really powerful guy. And okay, we never talk, and he treats me like I'm not there, and he only pays attention to me when I'm suddenly useful to him, like sending me to the monastery for the photo-op about how devout he is ... but he's still my dad. But maybe, when he sent me to the monastery, he was fulfilling a different purpose than he thought."

"What do you mean?" I said.

"I mean, I met you," he said, "and my eyes were opened."

"How so?"

"I knew they were putting up the wall. I knew about the international conference. I knew that it was all going to help my dad win the election ... but ... I never knew someone from the other side of the wall. That changes everything," he said. "Is my dad a bad man?"

I looked at the TV screen. I saw the Collector, barely meeting the rich man's eyes. I realized that this man, who terrorized me and hundreds of other boys, who had the right to beat me if I didn't meet my begging quota, he too had a master.

"The Collector works for your dad," I said. And then I noticed something else. "And the Collector has your dad's eyes. I saw that when I saw the big banner telling people to vote."

"Of course he does. They're brothers."

"But —"

"Different father," Lek said. "Well, it's just a rumor. Anyway, if you can't terrorize and coerce your own family, who *can* you?" And then, quite suddenly, he starting crying.

"Come on, Lek," I said. "At least you have — all this."

"That's the trouble! How can I sleep in this bed when I know now that every night you go to sleep on a pile of planks? And it's your suffering that makes these sheets so soft? If my dad really knew me, he wouldn't have sent me to have my eyes opened. He'd have left me blind." He was sobbing like a baby, he was desolate. I felt awkward. I put my hand out to stroke his shoulder, wondering if would recoil from my callused, lower-class fingers. But he didn't. He clutched them tightly and didn't stop crying, and I found myself comforting him.

And as I held him, I realized that though he had money, it was I was the stronger of us two. I felt protective. I didn't mind anymore that my mother had seemed to suck up to him and ignore me. I wasn't jealous of him anymore. In his own way, he was as deprived as me.

"I'm going to make it right," I said. "We may just be kids, but we're not powerless."

I fell asleep the minute my head hit the pillow and I passed directly into oblivion. Shortly before I woke, I felt the Stone Buddha's eyes on me again.

It was still dark when we left the house, but Sombun had already revved up the engine and in a few moments we were back on the expressway. I had fallen asleep in Lek's nice clothes and now I quickly changed. Lek slept in the car; he hadn't really woken up.

Sombun dropped me off by the wall; they'd bent the metal sheet back up again, but now there was another hole, near the bottom; someone had cut an opening in the corrugated iron big enough for a kid my size to squeeze through. I was just bending down to crawl through when Ake wriggled out, quick as an eel. "Oh, it's you!" he said. "Where were you this morning?"

"I saw the police so I didn't stick around."

"Let's go and meet Petch again," he said. "He's found a new corner to work out of."

I wasn't sure that I wanted to risk it, but Ake whipped out a roll of 100 baht notes. "I got your quota right here," he said. "Don't even worry about it. Let's have some fun and we'll split the loot."

I shouldn't have agreed to go. Perhaps it was because of the evening before, spying on corrupt millionaires and feeling suddenly liberated and empowered, but somehow begging didn't seem important. Ake had a way of bringing out my sense of adventure. He talked me into taking the skytrain, which is too expensive for the likes of us, but he the money. I'd only ridden it a few times in my life. It zoomed above the pre-dawn traffic; I could see the lines of buses, cars and motorcycles jammed together in the streets below. We got off and Ake amused himself by rushing down the up escalator, picking a pocket on the way.

"There's Petch!" He pointed and I could see Ladda, already with a crowd around her. This area was full of bars; they were supposed to close at two in the morning, but some seemed to be ignoring this. There was a different crowd from the hotel. The tourists who clustered around the elephant seemed a bit like zombies, glassy-eyed, swaying a bit. But they were still ponying up the cash to feed Ladda.

Some food stalls on wheels were already setting up for the dawn crowd. They would be serving noodles or rice soup as the buses began to disgorge all the secretaries, salespersons, and clerks that worked on this street. There was also a stand where they were deep-frying grasshoppers. I've never enjoyed eating insects that much, but Petch bought a bag as was crunching them by the mouthful.

"You don't see a lot of elephants in Bangkok," I said to him. "What happened?"

"We're all out of work," he said. "There's no more logging. They're protecting the environment or something, but actually they're just getting all the teak from Burma. I rode Ladda all the way from up north. Took forever."

That was the most I'd ever heard him say. I think he had been practicing the speech because it was in a passable version of our central dialect.

On the other side of the street, another elephant walked by, its skin glowing beneath fluorescent pink neon. Petch waved and the other mahout waved back. This wasn't like the elephant from the day before, the one who was trying to protect its turf.

Way down the street, I saw another elephant, too, this one gaily painted in stripes of green and purple.

"They're invading Bangkok," Ake said. "And they're driving the bosses crazy. No turf, no agencies, no Collectors ... all freelance. Bad for business."

"Good for us," Petch said. Someone was thrusting another banknote into his hand. An old foreigner and a young woman were leaning against the elephant while a friend snapped pictures.

"Not for long," said Ake.

A couple of policemen were marching purposefully towards us. "Is that elephant licensed?" one of them shouted at us.

"Let's make a run for it." Ake said. He grabbed my arm and shoved me up Ladda's side. I scrambled to hold on as Ake got running start and leaped up and was hoisted into position.

Ladda began to trot up the sidewalk. "You've got to be kidding," I said.

Petch said, "Don't worry. This girl's got a few good moves." At that point, Ladda started to *run*. I held on to Ake. Ake held on to Petch. You think elephants are slow, lumberin creatures? Think again. Those two policemen were sweating and swearing at us as we whipped around a corner.

"But they'll call for reinforcements — with motorbikes," I said.

"Never fear," Petch said. The elephant lurched into an alley, knocking over a cart full of pomelos and dragonfruit. The oddest part of it was that all the street people took this in their stride and just went about their business. A couple of tourists ran after us with their mobile phones set on video. Seeing their cell phones, Petch whipped out one from his pocket and began jabbering away in the northern dialect. The cops were catching up and it was a tight alley. There were open shophouses on either side, and the owners were just now, in the dawn, pulling up the metal shutters.

"Left," Petch shouted to the elephant, who careened to the left like a racing car, trumpeting wildly. "I've got some friends on the line. Get ready for a diversion." He put away his cell phone.

I could hear the roar of distant motorcycles. They must have called for help. The alley we were in had mostly shuttered shops. These shops have no doors; the entire front wall is open to the public, wide enough for a car or an elephant. The two policement were grunting, but they were catching up. This alley dead-ended into a canal.

We were two shophouses' length ahead. Then one. But at that moment, a shophouse shutter flew open and a couple of hundred chickens came stampeding out, flying at the policemen, tripping them up, sending them sprawling into a sea of mud and feathers. The shutter opposite opened just long enough for Ladda to lumber through, then clanged shut. At the back end of the shophouse, another shutter opened up. We were in the shophouse for all of ten seconds, long enough for me to see that it sold used tires.

Then we were through. In another tiny alley. A few doors down, man beckoned to us from another shophouse. "Through here!"

Ladda went bounding through and out the back way.   And now we were in a cool, tree-lined street, bordered by a green canal, with little wooden bridges up to each of the houses.   We got off Ladda's back and led the elephant deeper into the labyrinth of little lanes and alleys that branched off from the main road.

Ake had a lot of money and we were hungry. We stopped at a noodle stand. A few streets later we stopped for boiled chicken and rice steeped in chicken fat with a garlic chili sauce, and a few more streets away we gorged ourselves on barbecued red pork.   I hadn't had this much meat in months.   By noon we were wolfing down mangoes.

And somehow, by a route that had corkscrewed round and round, we ended up at my begging intersection, and I realized I had missed the entire morning section of my shift.

And there was the Collector was standing at the corner. he had obviously been waiting. I think someone must have tipped him off.

"This time, I've got you." he said.

He put a hand on my shoulder. His other hand held a bamboo cane.

I turned to my comrades, but somehow, they had known to bolt.

The Collector dragged me off to another alley, one behind the shopping mall, where there were huge dumpsters filled with the refuse of the rich.

He threw me against the hard steel.

"You missed work," he said.

"You shouldn't touch me," I said. "You know I've got powerful friends."

He started to laugh, and the feeling of power I had felt last night, and the excitement of the morning's elephant chase scene, all these feelings just sort of fizzled out. I knew he had seen me at Lek's house. I knew he had seen me at the prison. But something was different. He looked crazed.

"Come on, don't hit me," I said. "I know what you're going through. I know you're the boss's brother."

But that wasn't the right thing to say.

"It doesn't matter what you know. You didn't just not show up to work. You were with a bunch of freelancers. You were undermining the whole system. Don't you know it can all fall apart just like that? The entire system? With one little thoughtless act from one stupid little boy?"

"What are you talking about?" I said, defiant now. "Okay, I'm just a stupid boy. Beat me and get it over with and let me get back to work."

"I'll beat you all right," he said. "But you're not getting back to work. You'll never work again, not as long as I've got anything to do with it. Tomorrow afternoon at three p.m. all the international delegates are going to come down the street in a long convoy of limousines. They will see a beautiful wall covered with a beautiful mural that schoolchildren from a hundred schools have contributed to. And the press conference in front of the temple, the loving father and the devout young boy ... the Boss will be untouchable. And come morning it will be Songkran. All our sins and all our bad luck will be washed away. I might as well have a few extra sins to cleanse."

"Please," I said softly. I just knew the extra sin was going to be murder. The first time the Collector hurt me he seemed far away; he was only doing a job; this time, I knew he *wanted* to hurt me. He himself was under threat.

He gave the cane a few trial swishes in the air.

"Please," I said again.

"I like a nice polite boy." he said. He smiled, and then he started.

It had happened before but I didn't remember it hurting this bad. "The boss's son can take a shine to you, can spring you from jail if he wants, but now you're crossing *too — many — lines."* With each one of those words he lashed me with his cane. I was screaming. I was sure it could be heard out on the main road, but no one came. I couldn't take the pain anymore so I squeezed my eyes tight shut and tried to will my self into a distant place.

Bud — dho — bud — dho —

The mantra Lek taught me came to me. The blows that rained down on me were happening to someone else. I wasn't there. *I wasn't there!*

My soul was about to gaze into the face of the Stone Buddha.

Chapter Eight
Towards the Light

I drifted. The dream of soaring came back to me, the one I'd had in the prison.

Soaring over the expressway. The river a dark glinting ribbon. The Temple of Dawn silhouetted against brilliant sunlight ... and eyes in the sky. Weeping.

Towards evening, I started to come to. I felt water on my face. I was thinking, It doesn't rain in April. I rubbed my eyes and saw that it was a little boy, one of the beggars, squirting me with a water pistol.

"Songkran isn't for another day," I groaned. The kid just giggled.

I blinked. It was bright, too bright. I ached all over. I sat up against the dumpster. I could see dried blood on my arms and legs and I was sure my face was cut, too. I pulled myself up, holding onto the dumpster for balance. Then, without warning, I threw up. It was lucky I had the dumpster right there.

There was no point in working. Besides, I dimly remembered being fired. "You're not getting back to work." Did that mean just for the next day or so, with all these splendid delegates in their limousines? Or was I now permanently blacklisted from the beggars' association? Frankly, I hoped so. It would be good to be able stop all this, to go to school, to grow up to be a real person. The only thing that was stopping me was money. My mother just didn't make enough.

There was a reason the Collector had been so vicious to me. Those freelancing boys had to be a real threat.

It can all fall apart just like that, he'd said. *With one thoughtless act from one stupid little boy.*

What if the act wasn't thoughtless, and the little boy wasn't stupid?

I pulled myself together. I was going to go home, clean myself up, sit down and talk to my mother. Life was not hopeless.

It hurt to move, but I made my way to where the wall started, found the opening, and crawled through. I hadn't gone twenty paces before I realized something was wrong.

I took the muddy path past the Chinese lady's supply shop. The owner looked at me with this quizzical expression. She knew something. When I looked back at her she looked away. I turned the corner and saw. My house was gone.

You can dismantle a place like this in about ten minutes, and it hadn't been done carefully. The walls were flat on the ground, topped by the roof. My mother probably didn't know yet; she wouldn't be home from work yet. But my little sister should have been back from school already. I stood on the ruins of my house. I looked around. The people in the neighborhood wouldn't look at me.

"What happened?" I shouted. No one answered me. They were all avoiding me. "Where's my sister?" Still bruised from the beating, I must have been scary to look at. I kept shouting and suddenly I noticed that everyone had gone back into their shacks. There was just me, shouting into the steamy air. It was only then that I started to cry. I hadn't done that the whole time that the Collector was working me over. I mean, it was bad, but in a way I'd been expecting it, I understood it. I curled up on the rusty sheets that had once sheltered me and cried myself into a stupor.

Finally it was Ake who came. He was squatting next to me. I was embarrassed. "Get away from me," I said.

"No, no," Ake said. "Come inside my house. You've got to eat something."

Ake's house was more or less a real house; it had been put together from real wooden planks, not odds and ends like ours. It had electricity most of the time (and when it didn't, Ake was the first to clamber up that pole and reconnect it). I didn't go there often. Auntie Nui was already back from work, and that worried me because she and my mother worked together. She was sitting on a battered vinyl coach. The TV was on, too loud, and it was hard to hear what she was telling me, and it was bad news, very bad news.

"Now listen," she said. "Your mother won't be back for a while. The Collector sent for her, made her come back from the factory. He said that you violated your contract and that she had to repay what they'd advanced to her."

"What do you mean?" I chewed on a stale *khnom farang* that Ake had handed me.

"She took out a loan against your begging earnings to pay for your sister's school books."

"The Collector told her that she had twenty-four hours to pay up or they would nab your sister to work for the rest of your contract. So she came straight home, got your sister, and left. She probably went upcountry. Do you have people up there, people who could give her money?"

"I don't know," I said.

"Look, I've got enough mouths to feed, so maybe you can go sleep at the train station."

She went back to watching television. I was dismissed. I slunk from the house and, in a moment, Ake followed me out.

"You'll be all right," he said. "It'll work out."

I said, "How?"

"Hard to say. No way you're going to that train station. You don't even want to think about what they do to little kids there. Maybe you can work in a factory; I could get you a fake I.D. Or come with me and Petch and herd elephants. The police are going to ease off as soon as this international conference is over. We'll pay them off. If you don't like going freelance, maybe you can run amphetamines. I hear there's a lot of money in it, and they have to use underage kids."

None of these choices seemed promising.

"Then, there's the really drastic option," Ake said. "You could rob a tourist or a store, get yourself arrested, sent to an institution. They'll beat you, but you'll eat."

But I knew there was one person I could talk to, one person who might understand.

"I'll see you later," I said, and resolutely started walking toward the fence.

Maybe it was rash of me. I knew that Lek's temple was a long way down the main road. I didn't know how long. I knew that it was a long way beyond the entrance to the expressway. I was injured and hungry and although it was getting on for evening, the heat was still merciless. I started trudging. I would get there eventually.

Now I had reached the place where Nen Lek and I first met. The food stalls were doing a brisk business and people were setting sidewalk stalls for a night market, putting up awnings and huckster tables so that the already narrow sidewalk now became only wide enough for one person to squeeze through. They were unpacking their metal crates and piling the tables high with teeshirts, pirate DVDs, handbags, souvenirs. Nothing of interest to the likes of me. I just kept tramping on.

The sidewalk market thinned out. Here, the streets were lined with brightly lit cafés and expensive shops that people like me never enter. There were bookshops that only had books in English, and tailors, and exotic European restaurants. The traffic streamed past.

I walked on.

The neon banners were far between now. Here were shophouses, still upscale, but with signs in Chinese instead of English, and a different variety of goods: gold shops, opticians, lighting, antiques.   Not many beggars now, but every time I reached a stairway up to the skytrain, there'd be one or two of them, Cambodians I think mostly, usually children, sometimes with a baby in their arms. A baby brings more income, but you have to pay rent on the baby.

Eventually the skytrain stations got further apart. Walking was a chore now. It must five, six, seven kilos and I couldn't walk very fast; I was limping worse and worse. It was getting dark now and the street wasn't as well lit as I was used to. I walked past what looked like a huge park behind a rusted iron railing.

It had got dark and I walked as quickly as I could. For a few minutes, it rained; the warm water soaked me, soothed my bruises a little; I was grateful for it.

Finally, I came to the high walls of a temple. The gate was already closed for the night but when you're as thin as me, railings aren't much of an obstacle.

I was standing in the courtyard. A lone, low stupa stood there, cracked, covered in moss; it almost seemed like a giant hedge. The flagstones, too, were cracked; weeds thrust up from beneath the broken stones. The moon was full and the rain had already dissipated.   Against an inner wall stood mango trees and the scent of ripening fruit sweetened the thick air.   It was more intoxicating than sniffing glue because it didn't have the feeling of sickness and decay....

The courtyard was empty. The wall in front of me had another gate, and when I passed through I was in another courtyard. This one smelled of jasmine. There was a vihara. Inside there would be images of Buddha. But the door was closed. I didn't dare go in.

In the distance I could hear chanting and wafting incense mingled with the scent of the flowers. My flipflops were so worn now, my soles touched the paving stones which still retained the day's warmth.

How to find him? How many novices lived in this temple and where were their sleeping quarters? I crept further inside, to yet another wall and another gate; I could hear hammer blows and I knew that someone's body was being nailed into a coffin for the night; they do that after the lustral water ceremony, when the relatives pour water on the dead person's hands, then put him away in the box and send him down to the room where the dead are stored.

A skeletal temple dog ran across the courtyard. He was white in the moonlight. I shivered.

Temples have ghosts. The moon was full. I was afraid.

I had to hear a voice, even if it was only my own. I whispered, "Lek, Lek, come out, it's me, it's me."

My own voice echoed back, like the voice of a dead spirit. I tried shouting louder. "Lek! Lek!" No use. I went to the next gate, peered through the railing. Was anyone there?

Then I saw the procession. Four men carried a coffin on their shoulders. Men and woman and children, all in black, all solemn, followed them. Through the railing there was a pathway and the procession was coming towards me. They were carrying a dead body in my direction.

Right across from the gate there was a low wooden building with a double door. Two temple attendants ran ahead of the procession to unlatch it. When the doors swung open, they lit candles inside and I could see shelf upon shelf of coffins, each with a little photo of the deceased, each body waiting in the storeroom for its slot in the roster of daily chantings that could last for weeks until cremation. The coffins were stacked three layers high; there was a stepladder so you could pay homage to the ones of the top shelf. I saw one that must belonged to a kid my age. *That could have been me,* I thought, remembering the murderous look in the Collector's eyes.

A strange wind gusted out from the room, laden with a rotting odor than all the incense and perfume in the world could not have hidden.

I caught the smell of death full in the face, felt suddenly all woozy and weak at the knees, and I screamed, "Lek!" at the top of my lungs before collapsing onto the ground.

Again I drifted. It was a place of terrible darkness in which dead souls cried out, unable to be reborn. It seemed to me that I was wandering in that terrible place for an eternity.

And then came light ... at first just a speck of light, then the flicker of a candle flame ... drawing me towards it. The light grew. I cried out with joy. The light bathed me. The light was soft, like Lek's bed. I laughed.

A face, pale as marble, looked down at me.. At last I was gazing on the face of the Stone Buddha! Those were the eyes that brimmed with compassion. I blinked again. The white stone darkened. Deep furrows seemed to form in it and I realized that this was a human face, not a statue. It was an old face that looked down on me with a gentleness I had never seen before.

"Buddha," I murmured. The light of morning streamed in from a window beyond the dark face. There was a breeze against my cheeks — an electric fan.

I closed my eyes again.

When I opened them, the old man was smiling. "My," he said, "our little novice *has* been filling your head with ideas. I knew that he respected me, but to tell his friends that I'm the Buddha himself...."

And he chuckled to himself.

I sat up. Immediately groaned in pain.

"Don't make any fast moves," Lek said from somewhere behind me. "You'll rip out the bandages."

I turned. "Ow!" He was there. He was sitting on the floor, his palms folded together in the attitude of a pupil attending his master. The kindly eyes belonged to an old monk, and I knew right away that this must be the Abbot he'd heard so much about. "Luangta," he said, addressing him as *holy grandfather* as befit his years.

"Don't try to say anything," said the Abbot. "You said plenty when you were unconscious."

"I've never heard anyone talk so much in their sleep," Lek said. "I know everything that happened ... your mother, you losing your job, everything."

I wished he hadn't reminded me.

The Abbot said to me, "Now, Boy, there are many things you can do. You could take the saffron robe for a while; that option is always open to any male person, as long as they can truthfully answer the question, *Are you a human being?*"

"Of course I am," I said. "Who says I'm not?"

Lek said, "He's saying that because once, the King of the Serpents took human form and begged the Lord Buddha if he could be ordained and learn the ways of the dharma. But the Buddha saw through his disguise and said, No way; you have many, many lifetimes to live before you can be reborn as a human being. But because of your great faith, all men who seek to become monks will first be called Naga, Serpent, in your honor."

"What if I'm not ready to take the vows?" I said.

"You could become a *dek wat,*" he said, "and fetch and carry for the monks; you'd get an education, and you'd get fed."

"I'd miss Lek," I said, knowing that he had only had a couple more days before leaving the monastery.

"So that leaves the third plan," Lek said. "You're backed against a wall. You see a little door and you can go in and hide. That's what you'd be doing in this temple. Or you can turn around and defy them all. Swallow these." He handed me two paracetamol and a glass of water.

"Oh, Lek. I'm so helpless," I said. "Yesterday I felt I could stand up against the world. I spied on the Collector and your father and together we thought, we know as much as they do, we can even defeat them.

And then we had the chase scene with the elephant and the motorcycle cops, and I felt on top of the world. And then the Collector found me and showed me I can be squashed like a cockroach."

"You are only like a cockroach," said the Abbot, "if you let yourself be like a cockroach. The Lord Buddha said that men are to be judged by who they are, not by what caste they were born into. He walked away from being the son of a king and owning a whole country. He went deep into himself to find the truth. You see, he was a bit of a revolutionary."

"That was all a long time ago," I said. "If Buddha had been born today, could he have changed the world?"

"Such a deep question from such a little boy." The Abbot smiled, rose up; Nen Lek prostrated himself three times as he sailed away, his yellow robes billowing a little in the wind from the electric fan.

"We're going to find your mother and sister," Lek said fiercely. "We're going to bring down all this corruption, even if I end up begging in the street beside you."

"Don't say that," I said. "We're talking about your father. At least you have one."

"My dad will land on his feet," Lek said. "He always has."

But he wouldn't look at me when he said that and I wondered what was going through his mind and if he could really bring himself to do what had to be done.

"Brothers," I said to him, wondering whether it was too daring to say that out loud.

"Brothers," he replied, without any irony, and clasped my hand.

Behind him, through the open window, came the sunlight, haloing his soft features.

Chapter Nine
Parade

To take on the whole universe-as-we-know-it was a tall order for a twelve-year-old boy with no money. But when I looked at the different elements I had to play with, I could just about see a solution. All the pieces of the puzzle were there. I just hadn't realized that there was a puzzle to solve.

I didn't want to stay in bed any longer. It was almost noon and the Collector had said that the delegates' procession was going to happen at three.

I told Lek what I was going to do. He let me borrow his driver, which was vital for the entire proceedings. "Sombun just sits around all day anyway," he said. "My parents have their own drivers. You can use him."

My first stop was what was left of my house; I had to find Ake. I asked the shopkeepers and they told me he had gone to the internet café.

This was a rather grand term for it; at the back of the slum, where the real houses start, there is a shophouse that sells fruit and vegetables in the front, and has a couple of computers in the back, stealing their wireless signal from a very high-tech, high-priced *real* internet café across the street.

Now, in a *real* internet café, kids are not allowed to enter during school hours. But since this was actually a vegetable shop, it was able to derive almost its whole income from schoolboys playing hooky.

"Ake," I said, "you've had enough roleplaying today. I need your help."

"What happened to *you?*"

I hadn't looked in a mirror. I know I was a mess of bandages and scabs and probably a black eye thrown in, but I didn't care. I told Ake my plan. I knew he would go for it, because he was just the kind of laugh-in-the-face-of-authority type we needed.

"We're going to need Petch," he said.

"Where is he?"

"The police told him to take his elephant and leave town.   But I think they've got a secret hideout, those elephant herders."

"Where is it?"

"We'll never get there in time," Ake said.

"Try me! I've got a Mercedes!"

We were the unlikeliest pair ever to board a chauffeur-driven white Mercedes, and Sombun looked askance when Ake got in.

"I see I'm going to have to wax the seat covers again," he said.

"We'll do it for you," Ake said.   "But you gotta hurry."

"If you do it for me," said the driver, "the leather's going to be filthier by the time you're through with it."   And then he started laughing.   "This is going to be fun," he said.

Petch was sleeping under a huge banyan tree in a park, covered in a tattered *phakomah.*   Behind the park was an old warehouse or factory of some kind.   It seemed abandoned.

We woke him up.   He wound the *phakomah* around his waist and rubbed his eyes.   "Tell the police I paid them yesterday," he said.

Then an amazing thing happened: he and Sombun started yakking to each other in dialect. Someone's fourth cousin's wife came from the same village! They were practically brothers! That was astonishing to me. In the big city, people seem like strangers even when you've known them for years.

Ake and I could barely make out anything they were saying, but it seemed that Sombun already knew a great deal about the dark underside of his boss's activities, and that the more he explained, the angrier Petch got.

Finally, Petch said, "Listen, I'm going to contact the rest of them. How many elephants do you need?"

I said, "As many as you can roust up."

Petch borrowed Sombun's phone and made a few calls.

"Where *are* the elephants anyway?" I asked him.

He smiled. "You think Bangkok's so crowded that a few elephants can't hide?" He whistled.

From inside that abandoned warehouse came the sound of trumpeting.

The three of us split up. Ake went off to get hold of the idle, internet-café-addict crowd; Petch went in pursuit of the rest of the mahouts; and I took the car so I can reach the beggar's guild before it was too late. I knew they'd be cleaning up the streets in advance of the celebrities' convoy. So they probably wouldn't be at their usual corners. I asked Sombun to circle about the intersections and in the back alleys. He did so with glee, taking the corners at top speed, lurching and braking more like a crazy taxi driver than the chauffeur of a distinguished politician. It must have been a big relief for him to let his hair down.

I caught sight of a beggar at last. It was a really little guy, no more than six or seven years old, who usually was part of a family group, with a mother and a baby. Of course, he wasn't really related to the mother or the baby; it was a cosmetic match designed by the Collector for maximum impact on the "customers". The kid was standing in a corner all by himself and I wasn't surprised no one had told him to move; he was almost invisible.

I got out of the car and waved to him. He ran up, giggling. "All gone," he said in an accent I couldn't recognize. "All go away in big van. Five minutes."

Sombun said, "He's had them all arrested! What a piece of work."

I told the little boy to get into the car. He was so excited that I could tell he had never been in this type of car before.

"What are you going to do?" I asked the driver.

"Bluff," he said. He gunned the accelerator and wove in and out of the traffic. "I know where they're taking them." He turned down a tiny alley and we saw a police van. It was no much for Sombun and his racing car tactics and we were chasing them through the little side streets. The little beggar squealed as though he were on a roller coaster ride.

This chase scene may have been faster, but it was a lot less nervewracking than yesterday's elephants and motorbikes. In fact, all Sombun had to do was dash into one side alley and emerge from another; our quarry couldn't react in time and crashed into a tree.

It was a sacred tree, too, hung with magical cords and flower garlands; doubtless the driver of the van was going to have bad luck for years to come, and would surely never win the lottery.

Sombun said, "Stay in the car." He jumped out and stalked aggressively to the van. He shouted, "Let them go! Boss's orders."

The men in the front seat weren't in uniform. They looked suspiciously like plain old thugs to me. "Police," one of them said wearily.

"Do you know who I am?" Sombun shouted. "Do you know whose car this is? Do you know who's sitting in my back seat right now?"

Thank heaven for tinted glass!

Their driver opened the back of the van and it disgorged a horde of young ones, all bewildered and disoriented from the little chase scene and from being plucked from work. The van drove off quickly; I explained the situation to the kids and told them that this was finally their chance to get back at the Collector — with impunity.

It only took a minute and the whole gaggle was sprinting towards my slum.

In front of the fence, the schoolchildren were standing to attention. The murals were all done now — they had obviously been working day in day out to finish them — and they were impressive.

I wanted to watch our handiwork. They had already barricaded off several streets, but the white Mercedes must have the right stickets, because it got waved through every checkpoint. Sombun parked behind a supermarket and I got out. I was across the street from the wall. I walked to the escalator to the skytrain so that I could look down and get a better view.

So, first, the boys and girls in their neat uniforms, row upon row of them, kneeling on the pavement so that the delegates could get the best view of the murals. The murals themselves: everything you wanted to know about Thailand — at least, everything they wanted the delegates to know. Slender maidens with broad hats bending over young rice shoots. Children riding waterbuffaloes. Houses on stilts. Pagodas and stupas. Fishermen in their boats, pitching their nets into the sea. And everywhere, smiling suns with golden rays.

It was a beautiful sight. But my heart ached, because I knew that it was there to hide the slum, to hide my home. My neighborhood, which may have been makeshift and ugly, but was still mine, where the people looked out for each other and where kids played and where we were a real community. We should they be ashamed of us? I thought. Aren't I also part of Thailand? Aren't I also a subject of our noble king, protected by him, warmed by the same sunlight as the rich? I saw this wall and I knew that what we were doing was right.

Now came the convoy, a dozen black limousines, each flying a little foreign flag on the hood. Motorcycle cops came in front and behind, as well as a car with a siren. They moved very slowly, in order to enjoy the spectacle to the maximum. Over a loudspeaker, some voice was commenting in English.

The convoy came to a stop; drivers leapt out simultaneously, door all opened in perfect unison, and distinguished guests stepped out to look at the children's handiwork. They all wore dark suits; the women were in elegant business attire. I didn't know how they could stand to dress that way in the heat.

On cue, all the children performed the most elegant *wai,* bending heir palms together in token of the gravest respect.

That was the moment when all hell broke loose.

First, a line of slum children rose up from behind the wall, seeming to be standing on the edge of the iron sheets, or even floating above them. They started to chant: *Don't hide the slum! We're people too! Don't hide the slum! We're people too!*

The delegates must at first have thought this was part of the show. They pointed, they laughed. The policemen, confused, couldn't shout at the kids to stop, because they themselves didn't know if it was part of the show.

The chanting went on and on and finally someone said on a megaphone, "Children, get down from there, please, it's not safe," but still they went on chanting, and then one of the policemen got stupid: he fired a round into the air.

The schoolchildren ducked,   Some screamed. Panic began to spread.

At that moment, there was a big, metallic, groaning noise.

People stopped.   The fence — it was moving!

The galvanized iron buckled, bent, with a rasping, hollow clang. The fence started to fold back on itself and then the crowd saw why the children had seemed to be suspended in the air ... they were standing on the backs of elephants.

And the elephants had been harnessed to the wall.

And they were pulling down that flimsy wall, as easily as if it had been made of cardboard.

All at once, the big fence was gone. It lay on the ground like a corrugated river.

And behind the that metal pathway was the slum.

The crowd fell silent, held its breath.

The familiar smell of decay hung in the air now. The delegates watched as the elephants, at a signal from their mahouts, all knelt down on the ground. Now they could see the piles of garbage, the dwellings made of plywood and cardboard, the wooden planks that bridged the sea of mud. It was appalling ... but to me, it was also home.

Now the children got off the elephants. They weren't chanting anymore. The school kids were gaping. The delegates stared, some in anger, some with a terrible sadness; one of them, a middle aged black man, was weeping.

This was a frozen moment. Well, in my memory it certainly seems that way. Thousands of people, suddenly silent, in a still bubble of time.

Then, abruptly, it was over. On some unseen cue, a dozen drivers leapt back out to open doors, and delegates got back in, and as they drove off, pandemonium ensued once more. There were cameramen everywhere, stampeding into the slum, television crews, reporters with notebooks. If only my mother and sister hadn't fled upcountry — they could have been on the evening news!

I ran down the up escalator in my hurry to get to Sombun. It was only moments until Stage Two of today's big plan.

"No hurry," he said as I climbed in, all breathless. "I know a short cut."

Chapter Ten
Songkran

When we arrived at the temple, using a back alley and entering through a back gate, I had to walk past several pavilions as well as the storeroom of the dead before I found the way to the main courtyard which I had last seen in the moonlight.

I squeeze into the main court which was now crowded with onlookers. No one looked at me twice because there were several *dek wat,* boys attached to the temple, standing around; some of them were helping out, handing press releases to the newspaper people, giving them water. I looked like one of them — hadn't the Abbot even offered to make me one?

The honored delegates sat in chairs under an awning that had been thrown up, and they had special cooling machines that hummed and sent out blasts of cold air.

Once again there were television cameras everywhere. I remembered that even in their dining room, Lek had had a hidden camera. These people's entire lives must be lived on television, I thought. Also, there were rows of newspaper people, holding out tape recorders, jotting notes. And there were also distinguished monks. I saw the Abbot himself in a front seat, with a dozen other clerics near him. Waiters with trays walked up and down serving tea and cakes to the guests. Others presented tea to the monks on their hands and knees.

Lek's father was sitting at a table facing the guests, flanked by two adoring young women who were some kind of aides or secretaries. I was nobody. I was invisible. I was able to creep up quite close, just another invisible urchin. And so I heard Lek's father's speech. It was in English, so I couldn't understand a word. Where was Lek? Wasn't he supposed to be at his father's side, demonstrating to all his family's piety and love of traditional values? I wondered whether they had changed the press conference plans.

But after Lek's dad had spoken for a while, very earnestly and intently, one of the sweet-faced aides translated into Thai.

"... to draw the attention of the international community to the terrible problems of urban blight in Bangkok and the plight of the poor," said the translator, "we organized this little demonstration this afternoon...."

I gaped. Lek's dad was going to take credit for the entire operation!

"... we are delighted to take this opportunity to ask the international community to open their hearts ... and their checkbooks. Bangkok need your help," she translated, "and sometimes the media need a little jolt...."

I stood there, becoming more appalled every minute. I thought of my mother and sister, wondered if I'd ever see them again. I thought of how we'd managed to mobilize all the dispossessed children of the streets. And now it was all being magically taken from us by a smooth-talking politician.

Where was Lek? Had he caved in, was this why he wasn't sitting there?

Now the translator was going on about the beauty of Thailand, the warmth of its people, and the richness of the culture.

And I was burning with rage. But who cared? Who noticed a small boy trembling with anger in the corner when so many celebrities were there, each one shining more brightly than the next?

And finally it came. On edge now, I listened to the translator. Lek's father was talking about some idyllic childhood, about fields and orchards and about not forgetting his rural roots. And then the translator said, "And now I want you to meet someone who exemplifies the best of our values, and our our hopes for a brighter world. In order to help me, my son gave up his school vacation to spend time meditating in a monastery. Tonight, he will put aside the saffron robe and tomorrow morning he will wake up an ordinary little boy. But for the next few hours, he is a sacred person who has devoted himself to the universal compassion of the Lord Buddha. So I have asked him to come and say some traditional words of blessing. He's just a little boy, and he's very shy, but he wants to share what he has learned with you."

Applause. The cameramen all turned toward the little iron gate that led to the inner courtyard. Nen Lek came out, to the clicking of cameras and the oohs and aahs of the delegates, who were overwhelmed by the way he carried himself. His eyes were downcast and he walked toward the chair where his father sat. He walked with utter certainty and also with humility. Twenty-five hundred years of Buddhist history was in the way walked, deliberately, breathing deeply with each step, feeling the inner rhythm of the universe. When he reached his father, it was his father who clasped his hands in reverence, for even the lowliest novice is on a higher plane of existence than a layperson.

One of the *dek wat* put out a chair for Nen Lek. In almost a baby voice, he recited a mantra of compassion. The guests smiled. It was so charming, father and son. The mantra ended. And Lek just sat there, waiting for a signal, perhaps.

A reporter said, "Are you happy to be leaving the monkhood tonight?"

He answered, "Life is suffering."

That is one of the four noble truths which the Buddha taught. There was another unnerving silence.

Finally, another reporter asked him a question. It was a woman reporter, quite young. She said, "Can you share with us some of things you learned as a novice monk?"

Lek said, very softly, "I wanted to do this for my family, for my father. He told me that it would be a wonderful photo-op. He said it would help his career."

There were some titters at this. No one knew whether to take it as a joke or not.

"We always become monks to help our parents. When we take the vows, our parents are released from several lifetimes of reincarnation, and it brings them a few steps closer to nirvana. This was a more, um, immediate reason to help, but I didn't mind. I love my father."

More titters. I'm sure they were thinking, The kid's an innocent, he says things without thinking, it's cute the way he sees the world. But I started to realize that Lek had thought his speech out very, very carefully.

"My father wanted me to learn the lessons the Buddha taught ... compassion for our fellow travelers in the way of karma, understanding the hidden truths about the world. Well, I was a spoiled brat, with my own Mercedes, my own driver, two laptops and three iPods. My father was right to make me learn those lessons. And I have learned some of them. Of course you can never learn them completely, even after many lifetimes. But I think I've already learned some of the lessons too well."

Lek's father looked a little nervous. And the Abbot raised a knowing eyebrow.

Lek said, "I knew about poverty, but I never knew a poor person before. I knew they existed, but I never knew they could be my friends. I learned to beg, but I didn't know what it's like to *have* to beg. I knew you should make sacrifices for your friends, but I never saw anyone sacrifice *everything* before, and do it with a smile. I learned these lessons about Buddhism from my Abbot, but I *saw* the truth of the lessons for myself, when I met a street kid who doesn't even have a real name."

And then Lek went and told the entire story that I have been telling you, from the time I ran into him in the street until the moment he sat in that chair, telling them the story. And here's the odd thing: to me it had been a series of things that happened, one after another, random events in a random world; but when *he* told it, it was a *story*. It was the story of two boys from different worlds, who could never possibly have ever met or had anything in common or become friends — yet did. About how each boy opened the eyes of the other and showed him how much bigger the universe really is. About how they helped each other to uncover a terrible darkness behind the shiny world depicted in those murals the schoolchildren had been painting. And about how kids, who may think they're powerless in a big bad adult world, *can* act to change the way those adults see things. Because no one is truly powerless when he has friends, a good heart, and something he truly believes in.

I was crying so hard that I didn't notice that he had pointed me out, that all those cameras had turned on me. It didn't seem important that hordes of photographers were struggling get closer, to get the best shot. It didn't even occur to me that tomorrow I would be front page news, and that for many people the first image of Songkran, the Thai New Year, would be the image of a scabby, choked up little boy bawling his eyes out.

That night I slept in the monastery; I had nowhere else to go. Lek's father did not come to his de-robing ceremony. It only took five minutes, anyway; it was a simple formula in the Pali language, recited by the Abbot, and then, lo and behold, Lek was an ordinary boy again.

In the novices' dormitory, he shucked off his robes and took a long shower. Monks are not supposed to disrobe completely even in the bath, because of the rules of modesty; also, they must sit down whenever they go to the bathroom; they're not allowed to stand. When I heard water sloshing from the bathroom, and then the sound of a stream of water projecting into the toilet, I realized he was doing both, and having a good laugh about it all.

That night, the novice monks planned a midnight feast of cheese and cough drops. I remembered that these were permissible "foods" because of a loophole in the monastic regulations. Lek and I, of course, could eat real food. But there was nothing else to eat. I gorged myself. I crunched those cough drops as though they were hunks of meat. I stuffed myself with cheese, not understanding how foreigners could like the taste of something that smelled so much like rotten feet.

At midnight, a *dek wat* came to tell us that the Abbot wanted to speak to us.

We were led past many pavilions, past the storeroom for dead people, through an old graveyard. Beyond that was a very old vihara, not part of the temple's public area. It stood within sight of an old canal. The doors were open and there was candlelight within. Wisps of incense hung in the air and the room was bordered by old teak chests, carved with images of demons and angels.

The Abbot was sitting in the lotus position, beneath an altar. Most altars have a dozen levels and many statues of the Buddha and other figures, all covered with gold leaf, all shiny. This had a single image. The Stone Buddha. The image was far smaller than what I had seen in my dreams, and yet, in the candlelight, its shadows filled the whole chamber, continuously shifting and changing.

"Lek," said the Abbot, "there are many things I have to tell you."

Lek folded his hands and prostrated himself. Nervously, I did the same, although my body still ached a little and I was stiff.

"First, your father has left the country. He is in Singapore. Now, you must not blame yourself for this. It was going to happen. His finger was in too many pies."

"I've destroyed him, haven't I?" Lek said.

"Oh, no," said the Abbot. "I wouldn't say so. Perhaps you have even healed him. And you know as well as I do that there won't be a prosecution or anything like that. Money will smooth things over, but perhaps he will find less dishonorable ways of making his next billion."

"And now, Boy, I want to talk to you as well."

"Yes, *luangta*," I said.

"You are going to give up your current unsavory occupations. *All* of them."

"Yes, *luangta*," I said.

"You are going to school."

I wasn't about to ask who was going to pay for that, and how my mother and sister would eat. I knew the Abbot was getting to that. "One of the newspapers," he said, "has a fund that sponsors poor children who really want to make something of themselves. It pays for their school fees and books, but to stay in that program, you *must* study properly. No goofing off. And that same newspaper has sent someone to find your mother and sister. Be patient. You will get your life back."

I prostrated myself at the Abbot's feet. This was more than I dreamed possible.

"Oh, and ..." the Abbot said.

I waited.

"About your name. I'm checking the astrological charts. I've heard that you never received a real name. When your family comes back, we will have a little ceremony for that."

A name is a magical thing. Rich people get them from astrologers, or even get them bestowed by a member of the Royal Family. People like me get common names that are shared by hundreds of others. In my case, all I had was a nickname.

"If I had a real name," I said to the Abbot, "I'd finally be a real person."

"Oh, you're real enough now," the Abbot said. "But remember, the universe is an illusion; we are all shadows cast by the turning of the karmic wheel."

The Abbot eased himself out of the lotus position. He lit a candle. "Now," he said, "I want you to see something."

He held the candle up high. Both of us clambered up the steps to where the Stone Buddha sat. In the gloom, in the half-light from the sooty flames, the Buddha's smile seemed to emerge out of a dark void, like a crescent moon in the night sky. I felt the statue's coolness even without touching the stone. I saw the Stone Buddha's eyes, illuminated by infinite compassion.

And I could see the tears.

"One last thing," the Abbot said. "A parting gift for both of you."

He turned away from the statue. I wanted to gaze longer into the Buddha's face, but I sensed that one just did not do so. To see the Stone Buddha's tears was to step for a moment outside reality, into a time of legend, of miracles. I know that I if I looked again I would not see what I had seen.

The Abbot pointed to one of the teak chests. "Open it," he said. "Go on."

Lek and I heaved open the heavy lid, with its carved Garuda, the magic half-bird half-human which is a symbol of Thailand. Inside the chest were two impressive-looking water cannons in fluorescent green and orange plastic.

"Songkran is coming," the Abbot said and, without dismissing us, he left us to pull out our new toys and feel their heft and think about the fun we would have come morning.

Did I say fun?

We stocked up the car with pails of water and we ran up and the alleys, squirting students, old men, transvestites, old ladies, anyone who didn't get out of the way. We squirted people from the car windows as Sombun drove up and down the avenue. We were splashed a hundred times. Someone dunked a whole pail of water over my head from an upstairs window. On Songkran the water is a blessing and no one can be angry no matter how many times they get soaked. All afternoon, in the searing heat, we cooled off, and then in the evening Sombun took us to the places where the backpackers go, and there the water wars are wild and you really get drenched and covered in flour and you just laugh and laugh until you drunk with laughter, drunk on plain water. Happy New Year, Happy New World! You can feel all the bad things that have happened all year long dissolve into the great river that encircles the universe. You can feel the terrible things you've done get cleansed. You are born again, and again, and again, and again, until you are born as the person you want to be born as.

Lek's parents had run off. My mother was being searched for. Lek had the mansion all to himself. I had the city all to myself. We shared everything. For three days, the water flowed.

And then came Monday.

Lek was on his way to school. He wore a white shirt and a striped tie. His hair was combed — by the housekeeper — and his books were packed in a brand-new leather satchel. I was in the car, too, because I was on my way to the train station. Not to sleep there, as I had once feared, but because I was going to meet my mother and sister.

The reporter from the newspaper had tracked them down, and another newspaper had made my mother a small gift of cash so that she could restart her life. The Collector was in jail.   Petch and his elephants had returned to the north.

My family would not be going back to the slum.

Because of what we had done on the day before Songkran, the municipal government had decided it would move the slum dwellers into some nice, clean projects at the edge of town. Was this a good thing? I didn't know. I loved my old neighborhood. I thought of Ake shimmying up the utility pole, of the mean old shopkeeper scowling at us, of the kids sneaking off to the vegetable shop that was really an internet café.   Those things would always be a part of me.

I got out of the car in front of Hualamphong Station. It was an intimidating place, with tall columns and grimy walls.   I could hear trains coming and leaving inside. As I stepped down from the car, Lek whispered his cell phone number in my ear.

"You'll call me tonight," he said.   "On the weekends we'll get together.   We'll have adventures."

I nodded.   It was really just to make him feel less sad. Because I knew even then that it would not happen.   In the end, we were from different worlds.   We smiled at each other, and I thought, *I'll never see you again,* and turned away quickly because I didn't want him to see me cry. Once was enough.

I did see him again, though.   Only once. This is how it happened....

Chapter Eleven
My Real Name

A year went by.

Ake's family, like mine, was relocated to a government project. We became close friends. He wants to be a computer scientist when he grows up. My sister wants to be a politician so that her face can hang on a banner with a big number attached to it.

I still don't know what I want to be.

The slum had never really belonged to us; all the people in it had been squatting for over fifty years. The real owner was happy about the government project, because he didn't have to evict anyone; they did it for him. He transformed the land into a shopping mall with a bowling alley, a supermarket, and a multiplex. In only a year, it was unrecognizable and would not have had to be hidden by a corrugated iron fence.

The ladies from the newspaper were good to us; with the gift they got my mother, she was able to start a dressmaking business of her own, and with the scholarship they gave me, I managed to start school again, though it was a real struggle.

A call came from the monastery. Once again, it was the day before Songkran. It was an astrologically auspicious day for me to receive a real name, and the Abbot had consulted his numerology texts to find the right combination of consonants and vowels that would turn my life around. My family took a taxi to the monastery because the skytrain hadn't been built up all the way to where we now lived. The Abbot changed my name in his private rooms at the temple, in a small sitting room with one armchair, where he sat; my family faced him, sitting on the floor with folded palms.

It was just a little ceremony, set to begin at exactly 19:09 o'clock. It only took a few moments, but in those moments I became another person. I was magically reborn.

The Abbot congratulated me and then he said, "Look behind you; there's someone else here."

There he was, in the doorway.

In a year, he had grown a full head taller, and his voice had deepened. "I'm off to

England in a few days," he said. "They're sending me to boarding school there. So I thought I'd see you and relive some old times." He held out one of the water cannon we'd used last year.

The Abbot agreed to let us stay in a guest room in his quarters for the duration of Songkran. In the morning we participated in the ceremonial bathing of the Stone Buddha, and we also poured perfumed water over the hands of the Abbot, for good luck in the coming year.

Oh, yes. We had fun. We ran through the streets again. We sprayed all the passersby and we were splashed and dunked and soaked. We told each other stupid jokes. We made fun of people. We laughed and laughed and we swore eternal brotherhood again.

But a sadness ran through the whole weekend.

I know now it wasn't our friendship that I mourned. No, that was a celebration. The sadness came because we both knew we were no longer children. We were thirteen. We didn't live in the moment. We had futures to plan, journeys to make.

And when Monday morning came and when we stood at the bottom of the escalator where I was going to catch the skytrain to the end of the line and go on by bus to my clean and modest new home, and he was going to get back in his chauffeur-driven car and go straight on to the airport, I caught him studying my face, as if to make sure he would be able to remember it.

It all came rushing into my head at once. All the things we did. The elephants. Giggling at midnight. The cheese and cough drop orgy. Me weeping over the shards of my flattened house. The hidden TV camera in the vase of fake orchids. The laughter, all that laughter. I thought, I will never have a better friend than this.

We didn't say goodbye. We said nothing at all for a long time. We just looked at each other. Then looked away. Laughed again. And looked again.

Finally, Lek said, in his resonant new voice, "Boy, you never told me your real name."

"Oh," I said, "I'm too shy to tell you. I'm not used to it yet."

"You'll tell me next time, then."

"Yeah," I said, "next time."

I never have.

About the Author

Although S.P. Somtow is most well known for his horror and science fiction novels, and for having composed several operas, he has been producing fiction for young adults since 1986, when his fantasy novel *The Fallen Country* came out. The following year, his novel *Forgetting Places,* which deals with a teenage boy trying to cope with his adored older brother's suicide, was chosen as a "Best Book of the Year" by the young adult readers polled by the University of Iowa. He has also written, for young readers, *The Wizard's Apprentice,* winner of the Rocky Award for best young adult fantasy in 1993, and *The Vampire's Beautiful Daughter,* which was a selection of both the Science Fiction Book Club and the Junior Library Guild. *The Stone Buddha's Tears* is his forty-ninth book. He has also written scripts for animated series such as Disney's *Chip and Dale's Rescue Rangers.*

S.P. Somtow is a pseudonym for the Thai American writer-composer Somtow Sucharitkul. Born in Thailand, Somtow grew up in Europe and was educated at Eton and Cambridge. His first career was in music. His best known compositions are the operas, the most recent being *The Silent Prince,* and his *Requiem: In Memoriam 9/11.* His most well-known novels are *Vampire Junction* and *Jasmine Nights* which are both frequently on college reading lists. He has won numerous awards for his fiction including the prestigious World Fantasy Award, fantastic literature's most coveted award.

He commutes between his homes in Los Angeles and Bangkok.

Books by S.P. Somtow

General Fiction

The Shattered Horse
Jasmine Nights
Forgetting Places
The Other City of Angels (Bluebeard's Castle)
The Stone Buddha's Tears

Dark Fantasy

The Timmy Valentine Series:
Vampire Junction
Valentine
Vanitas

Moon Dance
Darker Angels
The Vampire's Beautiful Daughter

Science Fiction

Starship & Haiku
Mallworld
The Ultimate Mallworld

Chronicles of the High Inquest:

Light on the Sound
The Darkling Wind
The Throne of Madness
Utopia Hunters
Chroniques de l'Inquisition - Volume 1
(omnibus)
Chroniques de l'Inquisition - Volume 2
(omnibus)

The Aquiliad Series:
Aquila in the New World
Aquila and the iron Horse
Aquila and the Sphinx

Fantasy

The Riverrun Trilogy:

Riverrun
Armorica
Yestern
The Riverrun Trilogy (omnibus)

The Fallen Country
Wizard's Apprentice

Media Tie-in

The Alien Swordmaster
Symphony of Terrror
The Crow - Temple of Night

Star Trek: Do Comets Dream?

Chapbooks

Fiddling for Waterbuffaloes
I Wake from a Dream of a Drowned Star City
A Lap Dance with the Lobster Lady

Libretti

Mae Naak
Ayodhya
Madana
The Silent Prince
Dan no Ura
Helena Citronova

Collections

My Cold Mad Father
Fire from the Wine Dark Sea
Chui Chai (Thai)
Nova (Thai)
The Pavilion of Frozen Women
Dragon's Fin Soup
Tagging the Moon
Face of Death (Thai)
Other Edens
S.P. Somtow's The Great Tales (Thai)

Essays, Poetry and Miscellanies

Opus Fifty
A Certain Slant of "I"
Sonnets about Serial Killers
Opera East
Victory in Vienna
Nirvana Express